THE DEADLINE DOLLY

When Amanda Chester almost literally burst into private eye Dale Shand's Baker Street offices, he mentally catalogued her as trouble looking for somewhere to happen. But not even he could foresee the staggering shape of things to come. Shand is caught up in a network of intrigue and violence which swings him from London to Rome and on to his native New York, on a mission which takes in student revolution, murder and a nightmare date in a Mediterranean swimming-pool with a mako shark . . .

DOUGLAS ENEFER

---◆---

THE DEADLINE DOLLY

Complete and Unabridged

LINFORD
Leicester

First published in Great Britain in 1970 by
Robert Hale Limited
London

First Linford Edition
published 2002
by arrangement with
Robert Hale Limited
London

British Library CIP Data

Enefer, Douglas, *1906* –
The deadline dolly.—Large print ed.—
Linford mystery library
1. Detective and mystery stories
2. Large type books
I. Title
823.9'14 [F]

ISBN 0–7089–9762–7

Published by
F. A. Thorpe (Publishing)
Anstey, Leicestershire

Set by Words & Graphics Ltd.
Anstey, Leicestershire
Printed and bound in Great Britain by
T. J. International Ltd., Padstow, Cornwall

This book is printed on acid-free paper

To P. G. Wodehouse
for the unending pleasure
of all his books

1

She was trouble looking for somewhere to happen and I sensed it even before she crossed her mini-skirted legs and started talking in the slightly fluttering manner which made me think of Fleur Forsyte in the B.B.C. television saga. But the daughter of Soames Forsyte was rich and spoiled and Amanda Chester was an eighteen guineas a week secretary with a problem which seemed none of my business.

I thought she was in her middle twenties or even less when she arrived at my Baker Street offices without benefit of appointment. This immediately involved her in a minor clash with Nancy, who stands guard on the outer perimeter of the Dale Shand headquarters, now based on London. I could hear feminine voices joined in combat, then a silence followed by a flurry of footsteps and the bursting open of my door.

She beat Nancy to it by a short head, almost falling into the room.

'Miss Amanda Chester,' announced Nancy in a tone which blended outrage and resignation in roughly equal proportions. She withdrew with that touch of hauteur usually adopted by butlers who would prefer not to be held responsible for peculiar visitors.

Miss Chester fluttered across the fitted carpet and fluttered down in the clients' chair on the other side of my desk without waiting for an invitation. She wore dark brown hair half-way down her shoulders and a dark brown leather skirt half-way up her thighs; I tried to do a nice clean job of not looking at them and probably failed. Not that she was likely to notice; she had the general aspect of someone about to erupt with candour and volubility.

But having got herself into the inner sanctum her mood suddenly changed to embarrassment. Two words were all she could manage.

'I'm sorry.'

I took a new natural wood pipe from

my mouth and said: 'What for?'

'I mean I'm terribly sorry for breaking in on you like this, Mr. Shand.' She twisted her long slim hands together and went on: 'Your receptionist didn't like it, I'm afraid.'

'No, she would want to know your name and your business and consult me before letting you in.'

'I'm afraid I was — well, rather rude to her. I'm awfully sorry. Will you see me?'

'I'm doing that right now, Miss Chester,' I said dryly.

A small flush moved briefly across her oval face. 'I mean will you *listen* to me?'

There was an air of muddled urgency about her and I could hear the small alarm signal in my mind clearly warning me that Miss Amanda Chester meant trouble at cut-price rates. So I said: 'Since you're here, yes.'

'Thank you,' she said in a low voice.

'You can thank me if and when I've done something, Miss Chester.'

'I saw your name in the phone book,' she said. 'How much do you charge for your services?' Without waiting for me to tell her she went on: 'I can't pay very much.'

I put my pipe in a tray and said: 'We'll work something out when I've heard what it is you're worried about.'

'Thank you . . . '

'And assuming I agree to act for you.'

'Oh, I do hope you will. I'm so dreadfully anxious.'

'About what exactly?'

'It's my boy friend, I think he's in danger.' She looked directly at me out of large blue eyes with amber flecks.

'What sort of danger?'

She didn't answer immediately. The wall-clock chimed the hour; otherwise the silence was about as heavy as a deepening depression. Finally, she seemed to pull herself together and said: 'I think he's being used in some way by undesirable characters, Mr. Shand. Only he won't listen to me.'

'*I'm* listening, Miss Chester, but I don't seem to be getting much of a picture. Suppose you start at the beginning?'

'Yes.' A wedge of hair sloped down one side of her face She pushed it back with a

4

small, fussy movement. 'I work as a secretary at St. Crispin's College. John's a third-year student, reading social science.'

'What's he done — slugged his tutor or insulted the Vice Chancellor?'

Another flush mantled her pale, attractive face. 'If you're going to be facetious I'm sorry I came,' she stormed.

'I apologise, but we don't seem to be getting anywhere, do we?'

'And your time is valuable, I suppose?' she said bitterly.

'Valuable or not, I'm making it available to you. Suppose we get to the point? What's your boy friend's name?'

'John Franklin.'

'And you're engaged to be married, I take it?'

Her eyes opened widely. 'Goodness, you must be terribly out of touch. Engagements and white weddings and all that sort of thing. They're out of date, you know.'

'No, I didn't.'

'John says marriage is an atavistic survival, a kind of anachronistic slave ritual without relevance in the context of a modern classless society.'

I grinned. 'Is that how young lovers talk to each other in their more tender moments?'

She jumped up from the chair. 'You're insufferable . . . '

'Oh, come off it, Miss Chester. Sit down and let's find out what's bothering you.'

She sat down, slowly and warily. On the edge of the chair, as if she was ready to spring off it again any minute. Then she said, more calmly: 'We both endorse absolute freedom. We believe that a truly rewarding human relationship cannot be sustained within the confines of an artificially imposed clerical discipline.'

'For God's sake, don't make socological speeches at me,' I said.

'I'm simply explaining the stand we take against the restrictive conventions of a society whose entire basis we reject outright.'

'You're still making speeches and getting nowhere. What's the boy friend been up to?'

Her small anger went away. She looked

down at her hands, then directly at me. 'I told you — I think he's become involved with undesirable people, Mr. Shand.'

'What people?'

She hesitated, then said: 'I don't really know. John says they're a small group working, necessarily underground, for the social revolution. If that were true, it would be all right.'

'You fascinate me, Miss Chester. You mean it's okay for the boy friend to smash the very system which makes his own way of life possible.'

'You simply don't understand,' she said. 'But, of course, you're too old. You've made a bargain with the system, you're a conformist.'

'And an American as well, which makes it worse.'

'I didn't say that.'

'No, but if you're running true to form that's what you think, isn't it? American imperialist aggression, capitalist exploitation of the masses quaking with fear as they drive to work in their new season's model.'

'You're utterly impossible!'

'Anything you say, Miss Chester. But apparently you stand in need of an impossible conformist private investigator. These people your boy friend's got involved with — don't you have any idea of who and what they are?'

'I don't know, except that they're not part of the militant student protest movement or lecturers or in any way directly associated with the university.'

'A revolutionary group or cell of unknown background. What's your real worry about them?'

'My *real* worry?'

'Yes. Your conversation doesn't suggest that you're likely to be over-worried about the existence of revolutionary groups as such. So there has to be something else. What?'

She laughed nervously. 'I'm not telling this very well, am I? But you're right. I have sympathy with the current revolutionary aspirations, especially those of the student movement. But . . . well, I think the men John is associating with may be criminals.'

'Then you'd likely be doing him a

8

service by reporting your suspicions to the police, Miss Chester.'

'You can call me Mandy, if you like,' she said unexpectedly. 'I hate formal modes of address.'

I let that drift and she added seriously: 'How can I go to the police? They'd want details, proof even . . . '

'Not necessarily. The police may be interested if a criminal organisation has infiltrated into the student protest racket.'

'You have the most damnably maddening ways of putting things, haven't you? It's not a racket. It's an expression of frustration by the idealistic young with the social *mores* of capitalism.'

'Well?'

She fidgeted around in the chair and said: 'Anyway, there's another reason why I can't go to the police. I don't want to run John headlong into that kind of trouble and you can't expect me to.'

'Perhaps not. What do you expect *me* to do?'

She opened a white handbag and took out a small piece of notepaper and pushed it across the desk. Typed on the paper was a name and address: *Garfield Ellery, Flat 5, Brynton Mansions, W.C.1.*

Mandy Chester said: 'That's the only name I know. He's one of the men John is associating with. I'd like you to find out about him and the people he's connected with. I mean whether he's what John believes him to be or something else.'

'Meaning something outside the law, in a criminal sense?'

'Yes.'

'And if he is?'

'I'd need proof, or at least a strong presumption of it — enough to convince John that he's involving himself with undesirable characters.'

I didn't like the look of the job. I didn't even need it. I had a new industrial investigation coming up for briefing at the week-end, a major assignment which would probably take me half-way round the world, all expenses paid and a four-figure fee for a satisfactory completion. I didn't want to know about girls worried over militant student boy friends, did I? Besides, there couldn't be much in it financially.

She said: 'Please — will you help me?'

I looked across at her and was startled to hear myself saying: 'All right, I'll see what I can do.'

'How much?'

'I usually get up to £50 a day, plus expenses — which have been known to come high.'

'I can't pay that.'

'Well,' I said, 'it seems like a simple enough inquiry. I ought to be able to wrap it up in a day. Twenty-five guineas and petrol for my car. Will that do?'

'Yes.' She eyed me quizzically for a moment. 'I thought perhaps you were going to say you'd take payment in kind.'

'What — and you already spoken for?'

'You're appallingly old-fashioned. I've never been made love to by an older man. It'd be an experience.'

'I'll take twenty-five for the day's work,' I said austerely. 'Where do I report — not at the college, I take it?'

'No.' She gave me her address, a flat near Russell Square, and I said I'd be along there not later than nine in the evening. That gave me eleven hours, which ought to be long enough.

If I could have seen even two hours into the future I'd have slung her out of the office.

Maybe . . .

2

It was a block of newish-looking apartments within sight and sound of High Holborn. They had a tarmac forecourt with sleek cars lazing like shining beetles on the marked-off surface, and a flower border separating the forecourt from a paved walk which flanked the entire front of the block and disappeared round the back. A bit plushy for the heralds of the great social revolution; on the other hand, perhaps not.

I marched up a wide span of concrete steps into a reception foyer big enough to hold a plenary session of embryo commissars, not that there were any on hand. Instead, the eye noted an elegently curving walnut counter behind which were three elegantly curving receptionists. I approached the taller of the trinity, a cool brunette who looked as if she could warm up if the conditions were right. Just at this moment they weren't and she surveyed me with a kind of regal patronage, as might a queen condescending to notice the existence of a subject of plebeian origin.

'*Yais?*' That was exactly how she pronounced it.

I said, in an exaggerated hardrock pioneer voice like Uncle Elmer calling from the woodshed: 'Is Mistuh Garfield Ellery in, ma'am?'

She flicked a non-existent speck of dust from the matchless lace cuffs of her duty dress. 'Your name, sir?'

'Shand, Dale Shand.'

'You have a calling card?'

'Sure.' I gave her the one without either the crossed guns rampant or the specific nature of my work.

She picked it up as if half-expecting to catch Mao flu and studied it with elaborate disdain. 'Dale Shand, private consultant. What sort of consultancy?'

'It's none of your business, honey, is it?'

Ice formed on her magnificent upper slopes. 'I should prefer that you did not address me as honey,' she said.

I killed the overdone nasal accent and

said in my normal voice, which nowadays is tending to be mid-Atlantic: 'I apologise. I was just being mildly humorous or something. I hope I haven't annoyed you, Miss . . . ?'

'Paula Vincent.' She gave me a vivid smile wide as all getout; that shows you what a pleasant speaking voice will do. Added to a certain old-world charm, of course. Get along with you, Shand.

'I'm very happy to know you, Miss Vincent,' I said.

'Are you from New York?' Her own voice now sounded pleasantly modulated, no more affectation.

'You could say that.'

'Over here on a visit, perhaps?'

'No, I'm not visiting. I live here now.'

'That's interesting.' She used both hands to smooth her hips, which were worth smoothing.

'I find it so, Miss Vincent.' I lit a cigarette, blew smoke at the match flame and added: '*If* you would be kind enough to inform Mr. Ellery that I'm here . . . '

'But of course — if he's in, that is.' She picked up a crimson house telephone and dialled. I could hear the ringing tone over and over. Finally, she put the receiver down and said: 'Awfully sorry, Mr. Shand, but there seems to be no reply.'

'Well, this is a surprise call. You don't happen to know when he's likely to be back, by any chance?'

'If he's gone out he probably won't return until after six. Actually, I thought there was a chance that he might be in because I didn't see him go out. On the other hand he sometimes takes the rear exit to the garages.'

'The fire stairs?'

'Good gracious, no. There are proper stairs at the back in a place like this, you know.'

'Ah,' I said feelingly.

She put both elbows on the polished counter and cupped her chin in her hands, which were ringless.

'If you care to come back just after six I'll still be on duty, Mr. Shand. I don't finish till seven.'

'I'll do that, Miss Vincent. How would you like to step out with me afterwards?'

'My, you're a swift worker, aren't you?'

she said, but without offence.

'I've been known to get that complaint in reverse.'

'Really? You surprise me.'

'I'd like to.' I thought: what the hell's the matter with you, Shand, making verbal passes at apartment block receptionists? Then I knew what it was — the fact that she *looked* aristocratic. She wasn't, not really, but she looked it and that, for some submerged Freudian reason, was making me randy. Goddamn it, Shand, you're pushing forty. Yes?

A superbly-suited fellow carrying a fair amount of flesh and an aura of authoritarian arrogance drifted ostentatiously towards us. Miss Paula Vincent detached herself from the desk and said, raising her contralto voice: 'If you care to ring later, sir, no doubt Mr. Ellery will be in. Good morning.'

I raised my hat slightly, gave the management a gracious nod and went down the steps and out on to the forecourt, but not to my parked Hillman Minx.

A short distance along the paved walk

an archway gave access to a tunnel which cut through the block to the rear. I turned down it and found the back stairs and started climbing, but not far. Only half a dozen steps were needed to bring me to the corridor with ground-floor flats along either side.

No. Five was midway down the corridor and there was nobody around. Just the same, I had a sudden feeling that what I was going to do was something that would take a hell of a lot of explaining. On the other hand, I wasn't expecting to be called upon for an explanation. Besides, geting into Ellery's flat might even yield information which would likely be impossible to get by asking him questions.

I had originally intended making a completely phony approach just to see what the reaction was. It might be much simpler to take a look round the place. You're being crazy, Shand. All right, so I'm being crazy. It wouldn't be the first or maybe even the last time. I took a slim wedge of celluloid from my billfold and got the lock open with little more trouble than robbing a blind beggar.

The door led into a short, square hallway with a parquetry floor, doors to the bathroom and kitchen and, at the bottom, another door which opened on a lounge with a Chinese carpet, a massive dark green three-piece, a twenty-four inch television cabinet and a miniature bar. On one side of the room was an arch through which you could catch a glimpse of the master's sleeping quarters, looking as if they had been lifted straight out of the rotogravure colour supplement.

There was a faint fragrance in the air, like perfume savoured discreetly. Maybe the service maid used an aerosol spray, unless Garfield Ellery was queer or given to perspiring. What the hell?

I stood in the middle of the room, taking everything in. There was a light mahogany desk in the window recess with an imitation period telephone on it, the kind the G.P.O. reportedly don't like you to have. It started ringing as I walked towards the desk, causing me to jump half an inch off the fitted pile. Nerves getting edgy, Shand?

The ringing sounded like the Last Trump in the total stillness of the room. I unhooked the fancy receiver and said, indistinguishably: 'Yes?'

'That you, Ellery?'

I grunted and the voice, which sounded as Manchester as Johnny Know-All, went on: 'Right. I'll have to make it quick, so don't bother to chat. It's still Wednesday night, six o'clock, Askam Cutting at Shadwell, isn't it?'

'Yes.'

The flat-vowelled voice chuckled. 'A full meeting — Kesselring, Lapete, Bowles and us. The big deal. A hundred thousand nicker split down the middle and we're away. Right?'

'Right.'

'If you want me before that I'll be in Manchester while first thing Wednesday morning — but I doubt you'll need to bother. See you, then.'

There was a click and the phone went dead and I stood there wondering who he was and why he expected to share a hundred thousand pounds with Garfield Ellery and for doing what? It was beginning to look as if Amanda Chester's fears might be something more than girlish.

I went methodically round the room, putting everything back exactly where I had found it; but there was nothing. What did that leave me with? A fellow named Garfield Ellery believed to be corrupting or incriminating a militant student and linked with a bunch of other fellows who were meeting in a couple of days to resolve something worth a hundred thousand pounds split down the middle to Garfield Ellery and a man with a Manchester voice.

Meanwhile, I was committing a technical break-in or in danger of being found on enclosed premises for an unlawful purpose. Try to explain that away if Garfield Ellery walks in.

I started across the thick pile for the hallway on my way out, but I didn't make it. A key was turning in the lock and the small metallic click sounded like the crack of doom.

3

I had just enough time to slide round the bathroom door and push it nearly shut before he stepped in from the corridor.

He looked in his early twenties, about five-ten, and wore a polo-necked grey sweater under a crumpled suède car coat, dark blue jeans and scuffed pigskin shoes. He also wore a lot of hair; it stuck out in spiky curls above the collar of the car coat and rode down the sides of his face almost to his chin.

Unless I was making the widest guess, I was getting a slit view of John Franklin, reading social science in his third year and doing something possibly less respectable on the side.

He paused in the middle of the hallway and called out: 'You in, Garfield?' He let about five seconds drift by, then walked on into the lounge. I could hear him moving about and it seemed like a good opportunity for a little frank speaking

— but not immediately.

I poked my head out, craning it to the right. He had left the door into the corridor ajar. I tiptoed to it, stepped out into the corridor and thumbed the bell-push.

The strident ringing was followed by an exclamation, then the sound of him coming down the hallway. He yanked the door inwards and almost jumped when he saw me.

Then he swallowed and muttered: 'I'm sorry — I thought you were somebody else.'

'You did?'

'Yes, I thought you were somebody else,' he repeated.

'No, I'm not him — or is it he? My name chances to be Shand.'

He fiddled with his roll-top and eyed me uncertainly. 'Did you want to see Ellery?'

'That's right. I take it he's not in?'

'Not at the moment, I'm afraid.'

'You're a friend of his?'

'Yes.'

'Minding the place while he's out?'

'In a sense.' He hesitated, then went on: 'Look, I don't think I know you, Mr. Shand. Unless . . . ' He let the sentence stay unfinished.

'Unless what?'

'Nothing.'

'Unless I'm connected with Kesselring, Lapete and Bowles?'

He stared uncomprehendingly. The pupils of his eyes seemed to have shrunk. 'I don't understand what you are talking about,' he said.

'No?'

'I'm afraid I don't know anyone with those names. Who are they?'

'Just a bunch of fellows. Which reminds me — are you by any chance Mr. John Franklin?'

'Yes, that's my name. How do you know me?'

'I didn't until now. I just happen to have heard of you.'

He shifted his weight uneasily from one foot to the other. 'I don't understand this, unless . . . ' He stopped suddenly.

'Unless what?'

'It doesn't matter.'

'I think you were going to say something about unless I'm the police.'

That held him, but not for long. He gave me a hard look and said: 'You're an American, so you're not one of them.'

'I might be, Mr. Franklin. Let's suppose that I have some connection with the law. How does that affect you?'

'You're asking questions based on an assumption whose validity has not been established, Mr. Shand,' he said coolly. 'Why should it affect me?'

'That's more or less what I asked *you*. Does it?'

He began closing the door. I put one of my big feet in it and said: 'How do you come to be in Ellery's flat?'

'I'm a personal friend, I have a key.' His narrowed pupils flickered. 'I think you'd better remove your foot,' he said. 'You're committing a trespass.'

'That's right, I am. Still, it's in your best interests.'

'What the hell is that supposed to mean?'

'You're a student, aren't you?'

25

'You seem to know plenty about me . . . '

'A little. Enough to suggest that you get back to the lecture room and quit playing with fire.'

'My God, you've a bloody nerve,' Franklin said. 'I think you'd better get out before I throw you out.'

I grinned. 'I thought you lads believed in world peace and the international brotherhood of man. Or is peace divisible and the brotherhood exclusive?'

Twin spots of colour showed momentarily on his pale face. 'You and your kind make me sick,' he said. 'The Great Society — capitalist exploitation of the people and aggression in Vietnam.'

'You want peace in Vietnam?'

'The revolutionary movement of students and workers is pledged to it.'

'Then I must have got it wrong. I thought you simply wanted military victory for the Vietcong.'

'You make me . . . '

'Sick? So you said a moment ago. I'd think more of you fellows if you fought for the National Liberation Front, the way some of your fathers did in the Spanish Civil War.' I took my foot out of the door and added: 'Is Ellery supporting your movement?'

His eyes flickered again. 'You don't even know him, do you?'

'I haven't yet had that pleasure, Mr. Franklin.'

'Then what are you doing here?'

'I was hoping to meet him. Instead, I've met you.'

'Well?'

'If I were you I'd take a long look at his background,' I said.

'Meaning what?'

'I'm not sure, but you might find that it's less concerned with the social revolution than you think.'

I was starting to turn away when he said: 'You can't toss unfounded accusations around and just leave it at that!'

'Why not? You guys toss plenty around — generalisations about war and peace and the decadence of democratic institutions and all the rest of it, don't you?'

'It's not the same thing. I want to know exactly what you're implying.'

'Just that you may be doing yourself a considerable service if you watch your step, Mr. Franklin.'

'My political convictions are no concern of yours,' he almost shouted.

'I don't give a damn about your political convictions, my friend. What I'm concerned about is that you don't put yourself in line for a criminal conviction.'

I walked away down the corridor with the sensation that his eyes were boring into my back.

★　★　★

I got back in my car and drove to the office. Nancy gave me her bright smile. She was looking as if she had just stepped out from the shower, changed her clothes and fixed her dark brown hair; but, then, this is how she always succeeds in looking.

'Did you make any progress with Miss Amanda Chester's case?' she asked.

'A little, not much.' I told her what had happened, briefly.

Nancy tapped her small white teeth

with a pencil. 'I don't think it's the sort of inquiry you ought to be handling,' she decided.

'You mean on account of I'm now in the big time, taking on major assignments for vast industrial cartels and what not?'

'Partly that. Not altogether, though.' She hesitated, then went on: 'I sense something funny about this case.'

'Not funny ha-ha.'

'No. It's just a feeling I have. I think you ought to close it.'

'Why?'

'I just told you — it's a sort of feeling that I have. I don't think you ought to get involved. Besides, there can't possibly be much money in it.'

'There isn't.'

'I suppose you quoted her a knock-down fee?'

'Twenty-five guineas, to be precise.'

Nancy made a clicking sound with her tongue.

'That's only for a day's work,' I argued defensively.

'You mean you expect to round the inquiry out in that time?'

'That's what I thought. Now I'm not so sure.'

She stood up from her desk and said: 'Please don't go on with it, Mr. Shand.'

'You seem more than ordinarily concerned about me, Nancy.'

She coloured faintly. 'I'm always concerned about your well-being, Mr. Shand. In this case particularly. Don't ask me why because I don't know, but if there *is* something sinister behind it you ought not to carry on.'

I sat on the edge of the desk and lit a cigarette. I knew she was right. If there was anything criminal behind all this it was a job for the police, not a private investigator — least of all an American one operating in a friendly country. Maybe I should go along to Logan of the Yard and lay a few cards on the table. They didn't seem to amount to very much in a specific way, but Logan might know something that I didn't and be glad of whatever information I could give him. On the other hand, I had an obligation to a client; if I went to Logan I'd find it less than easy to keep

Amanda Chester's name out of it.

Nancy said quietly: 'You've seen Miss Chester's fiancé and given him some advice. That lets you out. You've kept your part of the arrangement. You don't have to do any more.'

She was still being right about it. I made up my mind. 'All right,' I said. 'I'll see Miss Chester as arranged and close the case.'

'I'm glad,' answered Nancy, simply.

Her eyes met mine and I thought, not for the first time, that some of these days I ought to . . . what? Not make an amorous pass; that was something I couldn't do, not with Nancy. I knew well enough what I ought to do. I ought to marry her, assuming she was willing. I thought she would be. But I'm nearly forty and accustomed to my freedom. What did that mean? Freedom to read in bed at night or not to go to bed, freedom to walk out of my flat and come back at any time I pleased. Freedom to go to bed with a complaisant partner if I could find one, which was not impossibly difficult. I couldn't do that if I married Nancy. But I wouldn't want to. I ought to ask her to marry me. For God's sake, you'll never find anyone to compare with Nancy, and you know it. Yes, I know it, but I'm not ready — not yet. Some of these days. But she might tire of waiting and marry some upstanding young Englishman. I felt a sudden chill, almost physical.

'What's the matter?' asked Nancy.

'Nothing, why?'

'I thought you made a little shiver.'

'Somebody walking over my grave, I guess.' I slid off the desk and walked into my office without asking her.

It was exactly one minute after six when I parked in a vacant slot outside the address Amanda Chester had given me. I rang the bell of her flat. Nothing happened. I sunk a thumb in the push and kept it there for a second. Nothing happened again. Well, maybe I was too early. Nine o'clock she had said and perhaps she hadn't yet got home from work.

I hung a pipe from my teeth and went back to my car. A girl came down the steps. I said: 'Excuse me, but do you know if Miss Chester is likely to be in shortly?'

She paused in mid-stride, turned and came up to the car. A fair-haired girl with greeny eyes, quite pretty.

'I beg your pardon . . . ' she began.

I said it again.

'I'm afraid there must be some mistake,' she answered. 'Nobody of that name lives here.'

4

I turned the car round and drove back to my office, trying to make sense out of it. There wasn't so much as a glimmer.

Nancy had called it a day and I had the place to myself. I went through to the inner office and saw what was on my desk. A single sheet of quarto paper and an envelope. On the quarto paper, in Nancy's small neat hand: *Miss Chester called and left the enclosed.*

I slit the envelope. Inside were five £5 notes and a brief letter: *Dear. Mr. Shand. — Thank you for your help, but everything is now all right. I enclose the agreed fee. Yours sincerely, Amanda Chester.*

The letter had no address.

Well, that was that. Case closed — or was it? I had a strong conviction that if I cared to poke around enough I'd turn up something or other, but it simply wasn't worth while. I supposed she had reached some understanding with her boy friend and now knew I'd met him and wanted to call the whole inquiry off. All that made some sort of sense; but I knew that at the back of my mind I was vaguely troubled, specifically about the meeting at Shadwell. A big deal, according to Johnny Know-All; for big deal read criminal coup. You're letting your imagination run away with you, Shand. Forget it and go out and buy yourself a drink.

It was at this point that I remembered I had arranged to meet Tim Lorimer, an American correspondent in London, over a drink in a bar just off The Haymarket. Seven o'clock or thereabouts, Tim had said. I still had forty minutes in hand, so I could walk it.

I ran an electric shaver over my face, combed my hair and went out. It was a fine warm evening in late spring, a time when London seems to look its best — well, maybe any place does at this period of the year. I walked steadily and more or less at peace. Nancy was right — I should never have taken on a damfool inquiry like this. I was batting in the big league, only a few days away from an assignment which, if not dramatic, was going to pay me more money in a month than I used to pull down in a year. Who wants dramatic exploits at twenty-five a day — and only one day, the way things had turned out.

Wonder if that meeting down in the East End *is* illegal? You're imagining things again, Shand. Oh, hell — forget it.

I had crossed into Coventry Street and was approaching Piccadilly Circus when I saw her just ahead of me. She was still wearing her mini skirt and walking with a sort of nervous energy, as if she were late for some appointment.

Without stopping to think, I quickened my stride. The sidewalk was pretty crowded and she was weaving in and out of the strollers. Then she made a right turn into a side street.

I hesitated. What the hell did it matter? She'd closed her silly little case and paid £25 and I had it, so why bother? I paused irresolutely at the mouth of the small street. About three-quarters of the way along it a coloured electric sign was spelling out something. I couldn't read it from where I stood, but I had seen the place before; a basement dump offering what was euphemistically described as a cabaret.

Miss Amanda Chester turned straight in under the sign and vanished.

I went fast up the small street. Two girls with half a ton of make-up on their brassy faces and figures nearly bursting out of now-you-see-me-now-you-don't silk blouses stood one on either side of the entrance.

One of them said: 'Like to come in, sir — lots of pretty girls.' She gave me a knowing look, phony as all hell, from eyes like unspeakable sins.

I went between the two of them down a short flight into a cellar tricked out with a shabby black and silver décor and little circular tables with padded seats. About a dozen men, mostly middle-aged, sat around with self-conscious uneasiness, like stolid provincial aldermen stepping out of safe respectability; if they were waiting for an orgy to break loose they were in for a long wait. The place was a clip joint for out-of-town suckers and you had to be one even to walk into it unless you were looking for something not on the menu, like Shand.

Another girl, wearing one gold leg and one black below a plunge neckline bodice, drifted up. 'Champagne, sir?' Without waiting for me to tell her, she put two glasses on a vacant table and another cutie draped herself in a chair alongside it, eyeing me expectantly.

'Ten shillings and, of course, you will want to give the waitress five shillings, sir.' She said it with practised ease. If you sat around in a place like this you could get through twenty quid faster than the Concorde working up to the sound barrier.

I grinned down at her, picked up the glass and said: 'It looks like sarsaparilla and probably tastes like nothing on earth.'

The girl in the chair stiffened. Her eyes darted at an angle, but before she could say anything I waved a five pound note, not so close that she could grab it, and said: 'A dark-haired girl in a leather mini skirt just came in here. This if you tell me where she is.'

'I don't know what you're talking about, mister.' She said it with conviction in her voice and a lie in her eyes. She patted the next chair and added: 'Sit down and have a drink and meet the pretty girls. You like pretty girls, don't you?'

'Why, they're not for sale in here, are they?'

Her eyes started darting again. I said: 'The offer still holds. The girl who just came in here. She's a friend. I want to contact her.'

The hostess didn't even answer this time. Her ranging eyes had found what they were looking for. I could hear him coming across the floor. I turned slowly. Maybe he wasn't the biggest man in the world, but he was in line as a contender. He had an expressionless face pock-marked down one side and a midnight blue suit from the sleeves of which a couple of oversize hams jutted.

'Anything wrong, Millie?' He didn't look at her and he let the words out in a soft purr.

I said: 'A young lady friend of mine, a

Miss Chester, came down here a few moments ago. I followed. Where is she?'

He smiled, a long wide smile full of nothing.

'You must be joking, sir . . . '

'No.'

He shrugged enormously. 'Girls work here, but there are no girls among our patrons, sir, as you can see for yourself. Why not stay and have a drink. Millie will be nice to you.'

'As long as I keep paying ten shillings for two glasses of near beer, you mean?'

The smile died as surely as if somebody had used an icepick on its occipital bulge. I went on: 'A Miss Chester came down here. I want to see her.'

'Nobody of that name came in here, sir. No young lady of any other name came. Will that do?'

'I'm afraid not. I think you'd better take me to the manager.'

For a moment more he just stood there, his gaze drifting up me, making an appraisal. I am six feet tall, fairly well built and in reasonable trim. He could probably take me, but not without trouble and trouble is something they don't want in places like this.

He tried one more time. 'I have already told you, sir — no young lady came in. There must be some mistake.'

'Yeah, and you're making it,' I said. 'Do I get to see the boss or not?'

'Bloody not, mate.' His eyes, which were curiously reddish, narrowed to slits.

'I could make trouble for you and whoever runs this dump,' I said. 'In fact, if I don't get some co-operation I'll make it rather quickly.'

He considered the point. He seemed to be considering it from every angle. The hush all around us was like something you could reach out and bottle by the Imperial quart. His vast shoulders started squaring. I knew what was in his mind as surely as if he had sent me a radio signal. He had his position as bouncer to consider and he had considered it and decided what to do.

'Outside mate,' he said. 'Be quick about it, or else.' A hard tight grin creased the corners of his battle-scarred lips as he settled himself for the climactic move.

What you do in these circumstances is watch their eyes. They tell you exactly what the fellow means to do. That left me no more than five seconds. Well inside the limit, I drove a short-arm punch with everything I had straight into his solar plexus. He doubled-up like a snapped jack-knife. A high wheeze gushed from his sagging mouth and his hamlike hands clutched at the agony in his middle.

Millie screeched. One of the waitresses dropped a tray. The middle-aged mugs, rising like one man, streaked for the exit stairs. I beat them to it by a short head and was walking away before any more bouncers could get through the mêlée.

I walked to the other end of the street, turned right and then right again. That brought me into a narrow parrallel street. As I came up a black Mark 9 Jaguar nosed out.

A smoothly shaven man with dark shining hair was driving close alongside him a girl was sitting.

She was Miss Amanda Chester.

5

She saw me from a distance of yards, but I might as well have been orbiting the moon. Then the car was swinging out wide with the sleek driver making an upward surge of gear shifts.

I got the number, but I couldn't check it out at this hour unless I went to Logan. Maybe that was what I ought to do, but I didn't think there was time. If I hadn't seen the tight panic in her eyes I'd probably have supposed she knew the owner of the place and was waiting in his Mark 9 because she wanted to. What I was actually left with was the conviction that somebody had virtually forced her into the car, maybe somebody like Garfield Ellery? If it wasn't Ellery I'd have to go to the police; better find out first, though.

But the Jag was out of sight before a taxi cruised round the corner of the street. I stopped it and told him where to drive. He snapped his flag down and said: 'Right, guv. You in a hurry?'

'Yeah.'

'You looked as if you might be,' he said composedly. He talked all the time, not so volubly as some New York hackies, but not far behind.

'We get all sorts on this job, sir. All kinds of fares from dukes and duchesses to blokes who want us to find them a bird.'

It didn't seem like a statement calling for a reply, not that he was expecting one because he went straight on: 'Some of the drivers used to pick up prossies and their clients and drive them around for fifteen minutes or as long as it took. What a way to get it, eh?' He chuckled. 'Lots of that going on before the Street Offences Act. That cleared them off the streets and bloody good riddance, if you ask me. Not that they've packed up business. Bit more discreet now, though, as you might say. You aren't pushing them out of your hair every few steps.'

He droned on. I was only half listening, making perfunctory sounds in the back,

44

when he said something which jerked me wide awake.

' . . . yes, it's better now from that point of view. But the West End's still a funny place at times. Bloody dangerous as well, especially driving a cab. You never know if the fare you've just picked up is a gangster with a gun. There's one right near where I picked you up — in Gosley Street. Bloke what owns the Golden Cabaret Club. A right bastard.'

I thought: You don't know I'm not one of them, my friend. Aloud, I merely said: 'You mean the clip joint, don't you?'

'That's a Yank expression, but you're an American, aren't you? That's it, though. Basement place what calls itself a cabaret. Cabaret my left bleeding foot. It's a come-on for drunken mugs.'

'And the fellow who runs it is a gangster?'

'Him and too many like him these days.'

'He wouldn't be a guy called Garfield Ellery, by any chance?'

Before the words were fully out of my mouth I could see his back stiffen. I guessed the hairs on the nape of his neck were rising like porcupine quills. Any second now he'd be expecting to feel a gun in the middle of his back, or worse.

I also saw him drop his left hand. Before he could grab the cosh or tyre lever or whatever it was he kept for personal protection, I said: 'It's all right, driver, I'm not one of his pals. I'm quite respectable.'

He brought his hand up. There was a woven-leather blackjack in it.

I said: 'I'm not carrying a weapon and I don't want your money. I told you, chum — I'm on the level.'

He let the cosh slide out of his fingers. Then he said harshly: 'You knew the name, guv — that made me wonder. I'm still wondering.'

'You don't need to. If you must know, I'm a private investigator and somewhat interested in him.'

'Oh . . . ' He made a left turn and said urgently: 'Don't get mixed up with that bugger, mate — he's dangerous.'

'I thought he might be. Do you know where he lives?'

The driver shook his grizzled head.

'I'll tell you then — he lives in the block of flats whose address I gave you.'

'Jesus Christ,' said the driver. 'If you're not one of his mob you'd better keep clear.'

'I have a little matter to discuss with Mr. Ellery . . . '

He half turned his head and said earnestly: 'Don't do it, guv — I'm telling you.'

'Look,' I answered, 'whatever this guy is he has a flat in a respectable block and it's my guess he'll think twice about trying anything there.'

'Its been done in unlikely places, mate — don't kid yourself.'

He drove on, rather more slowly as if he didn't relish the idea of reaching journey's end. I thought over his last remark. It figured. I could be sapped down in Ellery's apartment and bundled into the back of his Jag and dropped in the Limehouse Cut with a couple of concrete slabs shackled to my feet and nobody the wiser for weeks, if ever. But why should Garfield Ellery do that? He didn't even know me. Just the same, what the driver had said figured all right.

I leaned forward. 'I'm going up to his flat. Will you wait outside for me?'

He turned that over in his mind for a couple of blocks, then he said: 'Okay, guv — I'll go that far. What happens if you don't come out in fifteen minutes?'

'Dial 999 and ask for the police.'

'Yeh — ambulance service as well,' he answered gloomily.

We got there. The Mark 9 Jag was on the forecourt. I went through the archway again and up the stairs and along the corridor. I had decided how to handle it. I had been told by a mutual friend that Miss Chester, an old acquaintance, was visiting at the flat and, as I had important business with her, I was taking the liberty of calling. Beyond that I simply didn't know. Suppose she gave me another look of non-recognition? What did I hope to achieve, anyway? I didn't know that, either. All I had was a conviction amounting to certainty that something was wrong.

The door wasn't on the lock. I could

have walked straight in, but I rang the bell. Footsteps sounded and the door opened and I was looking at Garfield Ellery. Seen close up, he was as smooth as polished teak and as hard; about a hundred and sixty pounds of expensively dressed suavity betrayed only by the pale blue eyes, cold as ice cubes.

'Yes?' He said the word on a rising note of interrogation and a slight cockney whine.

I told him who I was and went on: 'I'm anxious to contact Miss Amanda Chester on some rather important business and a mutual friend mentioned that she was visiting you, Mr. Ellery . . . '

I stopped. He was staring at me curiously. 'I'm afraid I don't quite follow this, Mr. Shand. I don't know any Miss Chester.'

'You don't?'

'I've just said so. You appear to have been misinformed.'

'The information was specific, Mr. Ellery.'

'It may have been, but as I know nobody of that name it must be wrong.'

He said it with unblinking assurance; if I hadn't seen her in his car I'd have believed him.

As it was, I threw subterfuge to the four winds. 'My friend mentioned that Miss Chester was meeting you in the West End and driving here with you.'

I stopped again, this time because something showed in his hard eyes. A sudden small look which vanished almost as it came, a look I couldn't quite analyse, but I had seen it.

Then he laughed. 'There must be some confusion, Mr. Shand. I did meet a young lady in the West End tonight, but her name wasn't — what was it you said?'

'Miss Amanda Chester.'

'Never heard of it. The girl I met was a Miss Julia Holly. I merely gave her a lift.'

'A girl with dark brown hair and green eyes, wearing a leather mini skirt?'

He fingered his beautifully shaven chin. 'Yes, that more or less fits. But not the name. You'd better come in.' Without waiting for a reply, he led the way into the lounge. 'Drink?'

'No thanks.'

'Suit yourself. I'm having one.' He poured whisky, splashed soda water in it and resumed: 'Something a bit odd about this. You're quite sure about the name?'

'It's the only one I know her by.'

He sipped his drink and said: 'Bloody odd, but I certainly never heard the name before.'

'The girl you met, this Miss Holly,' I said. 'Is she here?'

'You're thinking it may be one and the same girl using different names?'

'It sounds far-fetched, but it could be, Mr. Ellery.'

I looked through the arch into the bedroom. He smiled and said: 'I dropped Julia off on the way here. She wanted to call on a girl friend.'

It was possible. The taxi hadn't tailed the car — I had merely guessed where to drive.

Ellery went on smoothly: 'As to the description, it could fit a lot of young girls these days, wouldn't you say?'

'Yeah, except for the fact that I was told she was meeting you.' But that wasn't true; I had seen a girl who looked like

Amanda Chester from the rear go into the clip joint and I had seen her in his car, closer. But I could still have been misled by a resemblance. Then I remembered Franklin being in this apartment . . . there *had* to be a connection.

Ellery put his glass down and said: 'Someone has been having you on, I'm afraid.'

I tried a final gambit. 'Does Julia Holly live in Carling Crescent, near Russell Square?'

Again there was a small rapid flicker in his eyes. But he answered immediately and with disarming casualness. 'To tell you the truth, I don't know her address. It's a new one. She had a flat near Mount Street until recently, but left it, and I'm afraid I haven't got her new address.' He got a smile out and hung it on his beautifully shaven face. 'Julia is — well, a girl friend. I never went to her place, but she sometimes comes here, if you take my meaning.'

'Very clearly, Mr. Ellery.' Everything he had said was plausible, but I had an intuitive feeling that there was something wrong about it.

The telephone rang. He picked up the receiver and said: 'Ellery here.' Then he put a hand over the mouthpiece and called: 'Excuse me just a minute, Mr. Shand. Make yourself at home — take a look round the flat, if you like, I'm rather proud of it.'

It was a tactical mistake. He *wanted* me to see that nobody else was in the place. If he didn't know Mandy Chester he wouldn't have gone out of his way to offer proof of anything he had told me. Inviting me to see for myseif was a give-away. I didn't even bother, beyond glancing into the bedroom. There was no sign of her, no feminine possessions, nothing that suggested anybody lived here except Garfield Ellery.

I could hear him answering the telephone caller in short sentences: 'Yes. I get it. Thanks for letting me know. I'll handle it at this end. Right.'

When he put the receiver down I said: 'Well, I'm sorry to have troubled you, Mr. Ellery.'

'Just a misunderstanding — not to worry,' he smiled.

'Yes, my friend must have got the facts a bit muddled.'

'Such things happen.' He walked with me to the door. 'I hope you manage to contact your lady friend, Mr. Shand,' he added urbanely.

Then I was out in the corridor with a head full of nothing that seemed to add up — beyond the sure feeling that he was lying like hell and making a good job of it. He had dropped Mandy Chester somewhere, but he wasn't going to tell me.

The taxi driver eyed me with relief. 'I was just starting to get anxious about you, sir.'

'Well, you can set your mind at rest now. I'm back all in one piece.' I got in the cab and told him to drive me to the bar — on the off-chance that Tim Lorimer was still there.

He was. 'I'd nearly given you up,' he grinned. 'What kept you?'

I was starting to tell him when he said sharply: 'Garfield Ellery . . . I've heard that name. But go on.'

I outlined the rest of it. He didn't interupt till I had finished. Then he said slowly: 'Ellery runs that clip joint you went into, but it's only a sideline. Your hackie friend was right in saying he's a gangster — and that's not all.'

'Well, what is?'

'He's believed to be associated with subversive elements — I hate that goddam phrase, but it fits.'

'You mean espionage?'

'So I've heard. Nothing specific because nobody's talking out loud — nobody in authority, that is. But there's a whisper going the rounds about Ellery being in with foreign agents either already operating in this country or from the Continent.'

I ordered two more Scotches and said: 'Is it possible that he's connected with some organisation exploiting student unrest in the universities?'

'I haven't heard that, but I guess it's possible.'

I remembered something else — the names mentioned by the man with the Manchester voice. Tim put his glass down

55

with a small bang. 'Kesselring is the name of a government official in Bonn who defected about a year ago. Some time later he turned up in Hanoi as some kind of adviser to the régime there.'

I sat hugging my thoughts. Tim dropped a hand on my arm and said: 'You seem to have stumbled on something.'

'Yeah — but exactly what?'

'This girl,' he mused. 'It looks as if she deliberately gave you a false name and address . . . '

'Why?'

'I don't know . . . wait a minute, unless it was a ruse getting you to contact Ellery.'

'It doesn't make sense, Tim.'

'It might — if she thought you were a threat of some kind to whatever it is they're doing.'

'Oh, come off it. I'd never even heard of Ellery until she dropped the name.'

'Maybe, but suppose she didn't know that . . . '

'She simply asked me to investigate Ellery to convince her boy friend that he was tangling with dubious characters.'

'So she told you, Dale,' said Tim quietly.

'It still doesn't figure,' I objected.

'Look, you can't even be positive that the girl you saw in the car *is* the same one.'

'If it wasn't her then it was her double.'

'That's possible, particularly in view of the fact that she gave no sign of ever having seen you before in her life.'

I breathed heavily. 'I guess it *is* possible — but the hard fact remains that Amanda Chester knew about Ellery. You can't argue that away.'

'I'm not trying to argue anything away, Dale. All I think is that you've become involved with something.' He eyed me directly and added: 'You've worked with British Intelligence in the past, haven't you?'

I nodded.

Tim said steadily: 'Don't you think you'd better talk to them?'

I looked at my watch. It said 9.25 p.m. 'I'll call them now,' I said and went across the bar to a pay telephone box.

Carruthers was on the point of leaving.

'You're deuced lucky to catch me, Shand,' he said. 'Had some rather important papers to go through. What can I do for you?'

'Frankly, I'm not sure, but I'd like to see you.'

'Urgently?'

'I'm not sure about that, either. It's a somewhat odd set-up.'

'I'll come along to your place as soon as I'm through, which won't be much longer.'

'Right, I'll wait for you.'

I went back and finished my drink, took leave of Tim and drove home. I put the Hillman in one of the lock-up garages down the side of the apartment block and walked slowly round to the front.

If I hadn't been preoccupied I'd have seen the man a split second before he jumped at me from the shadows.

What I saw all too clearly was something which looked like the Aurora Borealis exploding in light and pain which whirled off into a bottomless black void.

Shand went with them . . .

6

I could hear the drip of water, each drip falling with a tiny impact, monotonously repetitive. I got my eyes open and instantly shut them on an amalgam of agony and nausea.

For minutes I lay still, wherever I was. I was cold, colder than I ever remembered. I was lying on a hard wet surface with the damp saturating my clothes.

I moved a hand, spreading the fingers. They touched what felt like stone swimming with water. God Almighty — where was I? Better try seeing again. I tried, three more times before I could stand keeping my eyes open. I was in a cellar. A small cellar without furniture of any kind, without anything except one private investigator feeling cold, wet and ill. There was a grille high up on the wall and faint light came through it, as if reflected from a near distance.

Water was coming down the walls,

steadily and insistently; that was where the drip-drip was coming from, each drip hitting the flagged floor with a rhythmic plop.

I tried to stand up. My legs folded under me and I crawled on all-fours, like a sick animal. I put fingers gingerly to the back of my head. There was a spongy bruise, but no blood came away on my fingers. I was shivering, unable to stop myself. Time passed, about a couple of centuries of it. The shivering ebbed and with it the engulfing nausea. In the end I was standing up, far from being a well man but back on my feet.

Much good it was going to do me. I was in a tiny cellar with a locked door — and a ventilator grille you couldn't reach without a high jump pole and they hadn't provided one. They? Who were they? Then I remembered Garfield Ellery taking a phone call in his flat. It must have been a tip-off that I had been to the place in Gosley Street. I had gone in there asking for a girl who had disappeared and she had driven off with Ellery. For reasons I could only guess at, that made me dangerous; dangerous to *them*. The them-and-us syndrome or whatever the fashionable jargon is.

Or was I going crazy? How could Ellery have had me tailed? Well, why couldn't he? All he had to do was ring a number and have a trouble boy go round to my apartment and jump me. He had done it all right and I hadn't seen him again. All I had got was a fleeting impression of a sinewy man with a black sweater and a hat pulled half-way down his face and I only got that as he bore down on me with his cosh, hitting me as I jerked my head round.

But it didn't matter. Nothing mattered except getting out of here before they came for me . . . or left me here to rot. Maybe that was it. You could die here by inches and crumble into ultimate dissolution and somebody might find you ten, twenty or more years from now. A nice problem in forensic science for some police pathologist *circa* A.D. 2000. For God's sake, Shand, get a hold of yourself.

I almost lurched across the flags to the door. You might be able to blow it apart with an MBA rocket gun, but I hadn't got even a .38 police positive — private eyes in this country don't go around rodded-up, not if they know what's good for them. I stood there listening to nothing. No creaking sounds, no footsteps, no distant voices — nothing but the maddening drip-drip of the water down the glistening walls.

What time was it? My watch was still going and it said 10.40. More than an hour since I had left Tim Lorimer in the pub; it seemed like something that had happened in another age.

The faint light seeping through the high grille showed only part of the cellar. The far wall was a dark blank. I found it, moving slowly and with both hands exploring its surface. Nothing.

Where was the water coming from? I guessed the answer to that as the question framed itself in my mind. I must be very close to the river. I walked back into the middle of the cellar and stared up at the ventilator, which was wide enough to get through if you were 10ft. high and could smash the bars. The water was dripping a little faster down the wall immediately under the grille.

Suddenly, I knew what was going to happen — what *must* happen. The cellar was below the level of the Thames and at high water it was flooded unless somebody shut the gate across the grille and they wouldn't bother — not tonight. They had left the grille open and driven off, no need to stay.

I was going to drown.

I opened my mouth and yelled at the top of my voice. The sound seemed to bounce mockingly off the wet walls. Nobody heard. I hadn't supposed they would, but I had to try. I was in a disused cellar on a dark stretch of the river bank, a place where nobody ever came, even supposing anybody knew it existed.

The drip-drip accelerated. Minutes later the water was coming down the wall continuously. It would take a long time to fill the cellar at that rate, but it wasn't going to be at that rate — not much longer it wasn't.

I lunged back into the dark shadows, groping desperately — low down, just in case there was an open waste pipe, a trap door, anything. My foot kicked against something hard. I reached down and closed fingers round it. A crowbar, strong enough to kill one of them with, but not strong enough to smash in the lock. I tried, wasting my time.

Then it happened. The faint light coming through the ventilator almost vanished as the river swirled in, pouring down the wall in a cascade. Within minutes it was up to my knees. I staggered through the rising flood until I was directly below the grille. This was my last hope, the long chance — the only one I had. I pressed my back against the wall, feeling the river surge round my waist. It went on rising . . . and began to lift me with it.

I had the crowbar in one hand, clawing at it until my fingers hurt. If I let go I was lost, for ever.

Now I was treading water, rising all the time, up and up until I was within reach of the grille. I couldn't wait until I was precisely level — there would be no more than a few minutes before the water carried me to the ceiling and choked me.

I slammed one end of the crowbar between the bars of the grille and used every ounce of strength in a sideways pull, forcing myself back and back with my feet planted against the wall.

The water was swamping over my face, in my mouth and nostrils. I had no more than inches of leverage left. Half-choking, I lunged forward, pressing the whole upper part of my chest on the bar in the final, climactic pressure.

There was a single shattering crack as the entire grille burst wide open, the bars hanging down like smashed teeth. I tore at them with my hands, dragging myself bodily through the gap, already drowning because now the water filled the whole cellar.

My lungs were almost bursting under the dreadful asphyxiating pressure . . . but I was through . . . into the deep water of the Thames and swimming straight up.

My head shot above the surface. I gorged myself on air, gasping and half-laughing, half-sobbing. For seconds I was less than sane. Then, slowly, I began swimming for the shore.

Behind me lights glowed in a long line on the South Bank. There were few lights on the other side, which was where I was heading because it was closer.

A decrepit jetty thrust drunkenly out into the water. I climbed on it and half-stumbled ashore. A warehouse loomed in the dark, but no doors opened belching shouting men with guns.

I might have been alone in a dead world instead of somewhere on the river bank of the biggest city on earth. I walked down the side of the warehouse, came out in a cobbled alley and then on to a street. I kept on walking. Few people were about and they didn't seem interested. I found Stepney Underground station and went home.

A middle-aged man sitting opposite me in the swaying train said: 'You're drenched, I didn't know it was raining.'

'It isn't, I've just been for a swim,' I said madly.

He got out at the next stop and went into another section of the train. I went home to sleep and to hell with everything.

A shining black Humber Imperial was parked outside my flat. I walked up to it warily, catching a delicate whiff of cigar smoke. Ramon Allones.

Nothing but the best for George Carruthers.

7

He put his distinguished grey head through the wound-down window and said: 'What happened?'

'You'd better come inside,' I growled.

He closed the window, got out and locked the doors. 'You're rather wet, Shand.'

'Yeah — behind the ears,' I said.

'That I find hard to believe,' he replied genially.

I led the way into my flat and said: 'I'm taking a hot bath and doctoring the back of my thick head.'

'I'll do that,' he said. He did it expertly, adding: 'I have some surgical and medical knowledge. Bad bruise you've got. Not serious. Better see your doctor in the morning, though.'

'Make yourself a drink,' I told him.

'An admirable suggestion. I'll fix one for you as well.'

I ran the water, stripped off and slid

down in the comforting warmth. Carruthers strolled in with two whiskies, handed one to me and sat on the edge of the bath. 'Now then,' he murmured.

'I came here to wait for you. Unfortunately, I was so busy turning things over in my mind that I failed to see a fellow who was already waiting for *me*. I must be losing my grip.'

Carruthers touched his jaunty grey moustache. 'I also doubt that, my dear chap, but go on.'

I told him everything, in detail and in chronological sequence. He just sat there on the bath, sipping Scotch, saying nothing and showing nothing.

When I stopped talking he said: 'I'll fix a couple more drinks while you shove some clothes on, eh?'

'All right.'

When I joined him in my lounge five minutes later he said: 'You've bunged a spanner in the works again. It's getting to be a habit with you.'

'I don't follow that, but I'm sorry — if that helps.'

'Not in the slightest.' He crossed one

elegantly-trousered leg over the other and went on meditatively: 'You have a talent amounting almost to genius for getting involved in our affairs. It might be better if you gave up private practice and joined us.'

'Are you being serious?'

'On second thoughts, no. It's sometimes useful to have an unattached operator on our side. Besides, you aren't the sort of man who takes direction willingly. On the other hand, it would be a comfort for us to know exactly what the deuce you're up to at any given time.'

I stretched my legs before the imitation log fire and said: 'Suppose you tell me what the hell's going on?'

'It's a compliment to you that I'm coming to that,' replied Carruthers imperturbably. He put his glass down, leaned forward and said: 'This chap Ellery is associated with a foreign espionage group operating in Britain. A very unusual organisation. They're not accredited to any particular country east or west of the Iron Curtain. They're a small *élite* corps of free-lances whose

70

skills are available for anything from subversion to political assassination — at a price. There are certain — shall we say interests? — willing to meet the somewhat astronomical charges they demand.'

'And I've stubbed a foot in the middle of it?'

'Colloquially and admirably put, my dear Shand!'

I said: 'A girl is worried because she thinks her student boy friend is mixed-up with dubious characters and asks me to find out something about them. That's all I did.'

Carruthers permitted his left eyebrow to rise fractionally. 'I'm not criticising. You couldn't possibly know what you were getting into.'

'Are you seriously telling me that a gangster who runs a clip joint on the side is some kind of master spy?'

'Hardly, but he is being used by the organisation in some way which must seem important to them. We've been keeping an eye on him in the hope of getting a direct lead.'

You weren't keeping an eye on him

tonight,' I said sourly.

'It's not possible to watch him twenty-four hours to the day, Shand.' Carruthers finished his drink and added: 'This girl, this Amanda Chester or whatever her real name is. We know nothing about her.'

'What about the boy friend, Franklin?'

Carruthers moved his shoulders slightly. 'A militant student. Leader of a small inner caucus of militants pledged to the overthrow of the Establishment, the destruction of capitalism, democratic forms of government and conventional morality. Student power, the take-over of the universities, the dismantling of the examination system, international social-ism — student variety — and the ushering in of a new pattern of life at every level.'

'Who's going to arrange capital invest-ment, pay the rates and taxes, supervise production, salesmanship and all the rest of it?'

'They genuinely believe they can run the whole show. As to showing a profit in the form of a return on investment, that's an outmoded capitalist fallacy.'

'All this isn't new,' I said. 'I was in a state of intellectual revolt when I was at college. I simply grew out of it when I confronted the realities of life.'

'Of course. But it's gone beyond intellectual revolt. Now we're getting action. Sit-ins, demonstrations, fights with the police and all the rest of it. Also, a lot of these lads aren't so much Left-wingers as outright anarchists.'

'They're at university three years. After that they have to grapple with the real world.'

'Yes, but that's not the point. The real or imagined frustrations and aspirations of students can be used in the meantime.'

'By the group Ellery's linked with?'

'Exactly. I don't mean all students or even all the militants — but some without doubt.'

'You're working on the basis that John Franklin has been got hold of by this group.'

Carruthers nodded and I went on: 'He could've been persuaded that this group want to help his revolutionary student movement. There could also be another factor.'

'Oh?'

'When I was talking with him I noticed that the pupils of his eyes were contracted.'

'Drugs,' said Carruthers, 'and the hard drugs at that. Most likely heroin. H'm.' He made a small shrug. 'You mean they could be supplying him in return for services to be rendered?'

'Perhaps. But it may not be connected. We don't know.'

Carruthers fell silent for a moment, then said slowly: 'The names you overheard on the phone are significant, that of Kesselring in particular. He's the brain behind the whole thing.'

'Kesselring,' I said. 'That was the name of a high German officer in World War II.'

'Yes. The present holder is, of course, no relation. Also, it's not his real name, he simply adopted it. In fact, we don't know his real name — but to the best of our knowledge, he's half-German, half-Asiatic. An interesting ethnic combination.'

'I'd have thought a group of ruthless agents would have bigger game than stirring up the militant student business.'

Carruthers made a bleak smile. 'You're doing nicely, Shand. The target is something infinitely greater.'

'I'm listening.'

He didn't answer directly. Instead, he said: 'Corps One is the fancy name these fellows have given themselves. There are actually nine of them — a sort of Supreme Court of unattached espionage. Kesselring is the chief. Lapete is second in command. Bowles — who, by the way, is a renegade American with a term in Sing Sing to his discredit — is a sort of strong-arm man.'

'Well?'

Carruthers seemed to ponder. Then: 'It's understood that all this is in absolute confidence and that, if required, you will co-operate with us, as you did once before?'

'I've an industrial assignment coming up shortly. I may have to go back to the States in connection with it.'

'America, eh? Couldn't be better.'

'What's that mean? Oh, and you have my vow of secrecy.'

'Good.' Carruthers uncrossed his legs and said distinctly: 'The President of the United States may be making a British visit shortly. New talks to further the special relationship between America and Britain — which is rather more real than the cynics think.'

I didn't comment and Carruthers continued in a flat, dispassionate tone: 'We believe that Corps One will make an attempt on his life.'

'Are you serious?'

'The inner caucus of militant students will put on a very special demo and under cover of this Corps One will strike.'

'So that's where Franklin and his chums come in?'

'Assuredly. Of course, they know absolutely nothing of what is to happen. They will simply be helped to organise and finance a specially significant protest — that's where Garfield Ellery comes in, as link man between them and the Corps.'

'You seem pretty damned sure, but

where's the evidence?'

'We haven't got it yet,' Carruthers answered. 'That is to say, we haven't got it in the sense of its being evidence you could take before a court of law, but we know that these chaps have moved into this country and have made contact with the student group led by Franklin. For us that's rather more than enough.'

I lit my pipe and said: 'I don't see Ellery as a secret agent. He looks like what he almost certainly is — a well-heeled mobster. I'd have thought he'd be more interested in easy loot than political plots.'

'That's right,' said Carruthers coolly.

'You mean he's being hired by this gang at a price and because the arrangement happens to suit both their purposes?'

'Substantially, yes. Actually, I doubt if Ellery even knows yet what their real objective is. At this stage they don't want to show their hand in any way, so Garfield Ellery comes in as the link. He represents himself as the envoy in this country of an international revolutionary movement providing funds and tactical know-how to any militant group in the universities or elsewhere.'

'For God's sake, you don't think that even an extremist minority of students would be a party to assassination?'

'No — I've already indicated that. They will merely suppose that the organisation is sympathetic to them and is helping them to put on an exceptionally well-thought-out demonstration.'

'And when the demonstration is at its height one or more sharp-shooters with telescopic rifles will be in it?'

'That or something else. Our aim is to secure enough evidence to arrest the whole Corps before the Presidential visit.'

'I didn't even know there was to be one.'

'That's not surprising since nobody here, outside the Inner Cabinet, the F.O. chiefs and a limited number in the Special Branch, know anything at all.'

'Corps One seem to know.'

'Yes,' said Carruthers.

'Are you saying that somebody employed by the British or the Americans has leaked it?'

'We've screened everyone and they're all clean.'

'I don't get it.'

'Nor do we.'

'These fellows could be up to something entirely different, nothing to do with a Presidential trip.'

'We have that in mind, too. But the fact of their presence in this country at a time when a Presidential visit is under discussion is a coincidence we simply can't ignore.'

I got up, made two more small drinks and said over my shoulder: 'What do you want from me?'

'We'd like you to investigate the odd circumstances concerning Amanda Chester. That will put you in touch with Franklin again — and, sooner or later, will almost certainly bring you up against Corps One. They won't connect you with either British or American Intelligence — which will give us a useful advantage.'

I said levelly: 'You mean I'm to be the bait?'

'That's right,' rejoined Carruthers cheerfully.

'I could get killed.'

'There is that risk.'

'Ellery or somebody acting for him nearly got me tonight. Maybe next time he'll do a better job.'

'And that scares you?'

'Immensely.'

'Excellent. A man who isn't perturbed by the thought of mortal peril is either a vegetable or a fool. We have room for neither.'

'I haven't said I'm going to do it.'

'No, but you will. For one thing, you now have a score to settle with Garfield Ellery. Secondly, your fine old American patriotism is involved.'

'I hope Mr. President will be duly grateful,' I said dryly.

'He probably won't even know. Your satisfaction will be exclusively private, the knowledge of a good deed performed in the service of your country.'

'I never joined the Scouts,' I grunted.

'Their loss is irreparable,' said Carruthers gravely.

'Wednesday night at Askam Cutting,' I said. 'If you surround the place you might catch the whole gang.'

80

'I notice you said might. After your recent involvement they'll probably have a new meeting place. Even if they don't we still have no direct evidence. A lot of efforts are being aimed at getting it. It is at least possible that yours may not be without achievement.'

'You flatter me.'

'I never offer flattery. It is a luxury we do not indulge — among others. Specifically, if you get into some trouble with the law we shall almost certainly disclaim all knowledge of you. You will, though you scarcely require me to say it, be on your own. Well?'

'I'm in it,' I said.

Carruthers stood up and held out a strong, firm hand. 'You're a good chap, Shand,' he said. 'Better still, you're a born operator. Believe me when I say they don't come by the dozen.'

'What's troubling me,' I mused, 'is Mandy Chester. I don't understand why she gave me a false address.'

'No, it's puzzling, I agree. It's also important that we should find her. I suggest you see her boy friend again first thing in the morning. That way security doesn't appear to enter into it.'

'It doesn't sound a dramatic assignment, put like that.'

'You never can tell what'll turn up,' Carruthers said.

He left and I sat by the fire nursing my drink and wondering what the hell I was letting myself in for. After a while I got up and parted the curtains enough to look down on the street. A figure moved abruptly into a pool of dark.

I took a .32 automatic from a drawer and let myself out of the flat. The figure stepped smartly out of the shadows. An athletic young fellow in a dark suit under a short brown raincoat.

'It's all right, Mr. Shand,' he said amiably. 'Just keeping a friendly eye on your place.'

'Special Branch?'

'That's right. By the way, I suppose you have a licence to carry a pistol?'

'No.'

'It's a good thing you're not carrying one, then,' he said with a grin.

8

If the boy friend was at college next morning he must have gone into hiding because nobody recalled having seen him. But a fellow student, a clear-eyed young fellow with the fashionably over-long hair but no beard, supplied some information.

'He's out arranging some meeting or other. I heard him mention it yesterday. I'll give him a message, if you like.'

'I'll come back later,' I said. 'Incidentally, my name is Dale Shand . . . and yours?'

'Peter Guthrie.' He eyed me interestedly and went on: 'You're an American.'

'I cannot deny it, Mr. Guthrie. Are you by any chance a member of the Franklin group?'

'No. Are you connected with it in some way?'

'I'm a bit old for student politics, wouldn't you say?'

'I didn't raise that issue, Mr. Shand.'

83

'Well, you could say I'm interested . . . '

I broke off because a sudden small look came on his pleasant face. 'I'd better make it clear,' he said, 'that I'm not a militant and still less a member of this particular group.'

'You're here simply to work for a degree, eh?'

'Yes.' He compressed his lips and added: 'What's wrong with that?'

'Nothing whatever, Mr. Guthrie. I applaud it. I had the same idea at your age.' I grinned. 'That was long before students used the word amnesty to mean the exemption of rioters from the laws which bind everybody else.'

'Oh . . . ' He hesitated, then went on awkwardly: 'I thought for a moment . . . that is . . . '

'You thought I might be some outside contact of this group, whatever it is?'

'Well, yes. There's a good deal of feeling among some of the fellows and I have a certain sympathy, particularly over some aspects of university control and student participation, but . . . ' He shrugged.

'But you don't go along with this group, is that it?'

'Frankly, no.'

'Any special reason?'

He speared fingers through his thick hair and said: 'What exactly is your interest in this, Mr. Shand?'

We were walking slowly in a quiet corridor. There seemed to be nobody else around. I made up my mind. 'I think John Franklin and his friends are getting themselves involved with some rather odd people whose interests may not be what they are made to seem.'

'That's somewhat ambiguous, isn't it?'

'I'm afraid it has to be.'

He laughed shortly. 'You could be a police investigator, for all I know.'

'No, I'm not representing the police, British or American. Does that help?'

'I don't know. If you want the truth, I don't much care for this conversation.'

'Why, is he a friend of yours?'

'Not exactly a friend, but . . . well, I don't want to say anything that might adversely affect him.'

'*Is* there anything to say?'

Guthrie made another shrug. I dropped a hand on his arm and said: 'I'm trying to keep him *out* of possible trouble — trouble which could be rather more serious than organising a protest march.'

'I see — or, rather, I don't see. Do you mind being a little more specific?'

'I'm sorry, but I can't tell you anything more than that, Mr. Guthrie. But I ask you to believe that I'm quite serious. *Is* there anything else to know?'

'I'm not sure,' he said slowly. 'You mentioned possible trouble. All I can tell you is that John has been persistently neglecting his work and at the same time increasingly involved with some rather odd chaps — one in particular.'

'Describe him.'

He did it. The description fitted Garfield Ellery like the sixty guinea suit I had seen him in.

Guthrie said: 'I know nothing about this man or others John seems to be meeting, but I didn't like the look of him.'

'Did you tell Franklin that?'

'No, I didn't. It's — well, rather

presumptuous, that sort of thing, you know.'

'You said something about other men. Who?'

'Two others. I only saw them briefly. They had a car parked out the front.' Guthrie described them, but I had never seen them.

'Look here,' said Guthrie suddenly. 'If you're not from some official body you must be some kind of friend, surely?'

'You could say I wish Franklin well,' I answered. 'By the way, do you know his girl friend — Amanda Chester?'

'Slightly, yes. She's one of the secretaries here.'

'I'd like to see her.'

He nodded at a door. 'They'll tell you in there, Mr. Shand.'

'Thanks — for that and for talking to me.'

'I only hope I've done right,' he answered and walked on.

Less than five minutes later I was in possession of the information that Miss Amanda Chester hadn't turned in for duty. Rather less rapidly, I discovered that they'd called her number and had got no reply. I looked it up in the phone book: *A. C. L. Chester, Flat 14, Boughey Mansions, Earls Court.*

I went out of the college and got into my parked car and drove there. The flat was on the ground floor of what had once probably been the spacious Georgian home of a well-to-do family with a maid and a nanny for the children. The bad old days when students were less thick on the ground and none of them given to violent revolution. Now the well-off had long since vanished into the Surrey stockbroker belt or gone bankrupt under taxation and death duties and a new race of occupants was in transient possession. Among them young ladies like Miss Amanda Chester, university secretary and resident of Flat 14. Her name, typed in black with a red underscore, was on a card in a plastic-faced slot let into the heavy, brass-handled door.

I poked a finger at the bell and listened to it ringing and waited, which is something I seem to do a lot of whether

I'm in New York, London or any place else.

The door didn't open and no sound came from behind it. I went out of the entrance vestibule and down the side of the building until I was level with the living-room window. If anyone saw me I'd have some embarrassing explaining to do, but nobody did. There were red and cream vertical-striped curtains at the windows, not drawn. I flattened my face against a pane and stared into the room. A neat, orderly room with a faded blue carpet, a chintz-covered suite, a desk with books and papers on it and a sideboard carrying twin ornamental candlesticks, a bowl of fruit and a transistor radio.

The chintz-covered suite was ranged at an angle facing the marble mantelpiece but obscuring the fireplace itself. Nobody was sitting on the settee, but the spiked heel of a shoe barely protruded from the front of it, the part I couldn't see properly. Well, girls sometimes kicked off their shoes and stretched out before the fire. But there was only one shoe and for no discernible reason it interested me.

I tried moving sideways along the span of the window, but I could still see no more of the shoe. I looked up. A wide leaded light was partly open. I climbed up on the sill and wedged myself through the gap.

My feet made a soft thud on the carpet. For a moment I stood there, unmoving — not even wanting to move. But I knew I had to. I had to see for myself. Without any reason you could give in evidence, I knew what I was going to see all right.

I went round the end of the settee and stood looking down at her.

A day ago she had sat in my office with her fussy little Fleur Forsyte movements and now she was never going to make them again.

Her dark brown hair spread out over the carpet and her head was slanted at an odd angle. I had seen that once before, three thousand miles away. A girl with her neck snapped back like a flap.

Very dead. Like Amanda Chester was now.

9

I went down on one knee and put out a hand to touch the big neck artery. The exploratory gesture was automatic. It was also unnecessary, like calling a doctor. Better call the police, though. Or Carruthers. He had given me a direct line number, straight through to his desk with no preliminaries.

There was a telephone on a low bookcase shelf which ran along the wall from one side of the fireplace. I picked it up and dialled.

His deep, English public school voice came urbanely over the wire.

'Yes?'

'Shand,' I said.

'My dear chap, so soon?' There was a slightly abrasive edge to the urbanity now.

'Yes, I've found Amanda Chester. She's dead.'

'Ah,' he said. I might have been telling him the time. 'I assume you mean not from natural causes?'

'Strangled. Neck broken as well, by the look of it.'

'Where?'

'In her flat — which was not the address she gave me.' I explained what had happened.

Carruthers asked: 'Have you called the police?'

'Not yet. I judged it desirable to contact you first.'

'You're thinking well.'

'But the police will have to know, surely?'

'Of course, but I don't want you to figure in it — better if the chaps we're after don't know that you found her.'

'So that they won't figure I'm getting warm?'

'Precisely. Not that you're actually getting warm — are you?'

'No.' I said it perhaps a little shortly because we were talking about a murdered girl whose body lay within feet of where I stood and we might as well have been discussing some papers in the overnight diplomatic bag.

He went on in the same unruffled accents: 'You say you got in through the window. I'll have a word with Logan immediately and get him to send some men along. They can enter the same way. When the inquest opens they will have been acting on information received, which is a convenient phrase. Unless, of course, you have some imperative facts which must be disclosed.'

'None. I simply got her address from the university.'

'We can duplicate that inquiry as a cover for the officers.'

'Suppose I'm seen leaving here?'

'My dear Shand, I'm relying on you to avoid that contingency,' Carruthers said.

I hung up and looked down at her again. I wondered why she had given me a false address; perhaps because she didn't want me to be seen at the place where she really lived? If that were so then she must have been frightened of something when she came to see me. Frightened of whom — Garfield Ellery? But I had seen her going into his club, hadn't I? Going in to meet him and then driving off with him and looking straight through me, as if I had never existed. Suppose she had been ordered not to recognise anyone? In that case how did she get out of the car? There was an answer to that, though — Ellery had guessed he was being tailed and had simply stopped the car and told her to get out, which in turn meant that he didn't want them to be seen together. And I had gone to his apartment asking for her . . .

A cold sag gnawed at my stomach. The whole picture rose in front of me. Ellery dropping Mandy and going to his flat. Shand walking in, giving his name and asking for Amanda Chester. I had no way of knowing exactly what he had deduced from that . . . all I knew was that by going there I had signed her death warrant. I had killed her. Dear Christ, I'll get him for this, I'll get him if I have to travel across the world to do it.

It was warm, nearly hot, in her room, but the sweat crawling down the small of my back was zero cold. I couldn't look at her any more. She was staring upwards with the unseeing eyes of the dead, wide open. I wanted to close the lids and let her eyes have peace, but I couldn't do that, either. I couldn't interfere. The police were going to handle it and I wasn't supposed to be there. They'd drive up any minute now and I ought to be gone.

I went to the window. There were no cars on the fore-court and no sound of a car turning in from the quiet street. Just the same, better be on your way, Shand. I looked back for the last time and noticed that the right hand desk drawer was pulled marginally out. I slid it fully open.

Inside were three small notebooks, a stack of tinted writing paper and matching envelopes, a book of stamps and some gummed luggage labels. One of the sheets of writing paper had been detached and there was scribbled writing on it. I picked it up and read: *PADdington 089716 — may be important.*

Important for whom or what? I didn't know. I levered myself through the window, looking both ways. I walked without haste to my car and was three-quarters of the way down the quiet street when an all-white squad car and a panda drove in with their blue roof lights whirling. Plain-clothed and uniformed branch men were packed inside. They didn't even look at me. I turned out of the street, drove a short distance, found a telephone kiosk and dialled the Paddington number.

A woman's voice answered. 'Dr. Pascall's clinic. Good morning.'

'I'd like to speak to the doctor, if I may.'

'Is he expecting your call?'

'No.'

'Dr. Pascall does not speak to or see anyone without an appointment.'

'Tell him my name is Shand and that I'm a friend of Miss Amanda Chester.'

'Excuse me one moment, please.' There was a small wait, then her voice was back: 'We have no Miss Chester on the records, sir.'

I thought fast and said: 'But perhaps Mr. John Franklin is?'

Another wait, slightly longer. Then the voice asking carefully: 'You have been recommended by Mr. Franklin, sir?'

'Indirectly. The suggestion came from him — but through Miss Chester.'

'I see. Please hold on another moment.'

I held on, remembering the contracted pupils of Franklin's eyes. I had a pretty good idea what was going on at Dr. Pascall's place. Then the woman was back again. 'Dr. Pascall will see you in an hour and a half — at twelve noon, Mr. Shand.'

'I'll be there,' I said.

I drove to my office. Nancy eyed me meditatively. 'You're late this morning, Mr. Shand.'

'Late at the office, but not for work. Some rather odd things have been happening.'

'Concerning Miss Amanda Chester?'

'The late Miss Chester.'

Nancy's eyes widened, but she made no comment until I had told her everything. Then a small shiver rippled through her. 'How horrible,' she said in a low voice.

'Yes, it is.'

Nancy said slowly: 'You've got yourself into something now, haven't you?'

'It looks like it.'

We were in my private office and she was sitting on the edge of the wide desk. 'I wish you hadn't,' she said simply.

'If I'd taken your advice I wouldn't be mixed up in it, Nancy.'

'As a matter of fact, you did take it.'

'Yeah, but not when she consulted me.'

'I hadn't said anything at that stage.'

'You conveyed it, though.'

'Did I?'

'I can always tell what you're thinking even before you say it.'

'My goodness, I'll have to be careful, then. Actually, all I thought at the time was that there was nothing in Miss Chester's case for you.'

'Next time I'd better heed what you think, then.'

'You won't,' she said calmly. 'I think you have an instinct for trouble.'

'Meaning I'm enjoying all this?'

'Of course not — but drawn to it, yes. It's the sort of case that fascinates you, irrespective of whether you make a dollar for your trouble. Which reminds me, you have a highly-paid commission coming up and you simply can't afford to turn it in.'

'I haven't said I'm doing that.'

'You have five days left. This dreadful business could run into weeks.'

'I don't think it will.'

'You can't be sure of that and you know it.'

'Let's not meet difficulties before they arise,' I said. 'In any case. I may be able to combine two inquiries in the sense that both may require my temporary absence in the States.'

'You're trying to do too much,' rejoined Nancy.

'We'll see.'

'I wish . . . oh, never mind.'

'You wish I'd settle for the well-paid smooth angles of the investigating business, don't you?'

Nancy smiled. 'No, not really. It'd be out of character. You'd lose the qualities that make you what you are.'

'Which is?'

'Oh, get along with you,' said Nancy. She looked at her watch. 'If you're going to make that appointment you'd better be on your way.'

I looked across the desk at her. It seemed to embarrass her slightly. She slid straight off it and went back into the outer office.

Fifteen minutes later I managed to park outside the tall, old-fashioned house in Paddington where Dr. Pascall was holed-up. His rooms were half-way down an uncarpeted corridor whose musty aroma suggested dry rot in the skirting-boards. There was a small outer room with four straight-backed chairs and a low oblong table piled with well-thumbed magazines of the required vintage. Let into a wall was a frosted glass panel with the legend *Inquiries* in flaked black lettering and a tarnished bell which made a sort of jagged whirring when pressed.

The panel slid open and a woman of about forty with a sharp face and tinted blonde hair said: 'Yes?'

'Dale Shand. I spoke to you on the telephone.'

'Oh, yes.' She moved sideways, opened the door and said: 'If you will follow me, Mr. Shand.'

We went across her room to another

door with *Dr. Paul G. Pascall* inscribed on it. No letters after the name.

'Mr. Shand, Doctor.' She stood aside and I walked in. The room was high, wide and not handsome, though Dr. Pascall was. Six feet of slimly-built early middle age with a light face tan, bright grey eyes and clustering hair with a becoming hint of grey at the temples. He was wearing a pearl-grey suit cut by a supreme master of the craft and the simple dark blue silk tie was held against a flawless white shirt by a gold clip with a small diamond at dead centre. He had the general aspect of a sky-priced specialist in Harley Street and he was operating in a shabby old house in Paddington.

I stepped up to his desk and said without preamble: 'I believe you provide rather special services to suitable patients, Doctor.'

His clear grey eyes surveyed me thoughtfully. 'If you are a friend of Mr. Franklin's and vouched for by him that could perhaps be arranged,' he said.

I took a seat facing him and glanced

round the office. Everything seemed oddly at variance with his elegant appearance; shabby carpet, shabby filing cabinets, shabby glass-fronted fitments containing medical and surgical gear. Any way you looked at it, a lot of shabbiness. The ideas I already had about Dr. Pascall became certainties.

He leaned back in his padded chair, tipping his beautifully manicured fingers together like a pyramid. 'What is the specific nature of your trouble, Mr. Shand?' he inquired suavely.

'Something you can fix quite easily, Doctor.' I grinned at him. 'Fix is the operative word.'

'Indeed?' He was watching me, making a professional appraisal. A smile hovered briefly on his lean mouth and went away. 'If you will permit the observation, you have the look of a man in excellent health.'

'And as such in no need of medical treatment?'

'So I should be disposed to imagine.'

'Suppose we substitute inclination for need?'

He stood up, a fine slim man with a touch of controlled anger on his handsome face. 'I think,' he said evenly, 'I think I must bid you good day, Mr. Shand.'

I said evenly: 'Paul Godfrey Pascall, M.R.C.P., in single practice at Bayswater. No Paddington address or phone number listed. The number here is in the name of Agnes M. Southey, whom I take to be your receptionist or secretary. Interesting. Even suggestive, Doctor.'

He sat down slowly, making an urbane face, but he couldn't mask his eyes. They were both wary and uneasy.

'I took the trouble to investigate your background to a limited extent, Doctor. You run this clinic in your secretary's name and presumably attend here only at certain periods of the day. Any calls coming through here presuppose knowledge of the set-up. Your public image is that of respectable general practitioner. Your private image is — how would you describe it?'

He sat there watching me, wrestling with his thoughts. Finally, he seemed to come to a decision and said: 'What exactly are you?'

'A detective.'

The smile returned, not hovering this time. 'Your accent has American inflexions, Mr. Shand. I have yet to hear of citizens of the United States being enrolled in the Metropolitan Police.'

'I won't try to fool you, Doctor. I'm a private investigator and my interest is primarily in a young lady named Amanda Chester who is the fiancée of John Franklin.'

'I see . . . '

'Miss Chester consulted me about a certain situation affecting her boy friend. I made some inquiries on her behalf. They led me to you.'

'And you imagine that I shall sit here and submit to an interrogation?'

'I hope you will, Doctor.'

'My dear Mr. Shand,' he said distinctly, 'I am under no obligation to answer any questions from you.'

'But you will, though.'

'I beg your pardon . . . '

'I mean it's likely to be better for you to

answer questions from a private detective than from a police detective.'

That held him. You could almost see the shape of his thoughts, all of them disagreeable. I said: 'Let's quit playing games, Doctor. I have a shrewd idea of what you use this place for, but I don't have to tell the police. All I want is some information which I shall not use against you.'

Dr. Pascall fingered the diamond tie-clip and said harshly: 'You could have told me that in the first place.'

'I had to be reasonably sure that you were up to something. Your recent manner provided enough confirmation. You're a general practitioner who provides a drugs service on the side. Right?'

'I — ah — help the unfortunate.'

'Meaning you oblige anybody who wants a fix if they're safely introduced and have the money — in cash?'

'I dislike your way of putting it intensely,' he snapped.

'It checks, though, doesn't it? Unlimited prescriptions for addicts and no questions asked.' I glanced again at the glass-fronted fitments. 'Also, unless I'm making a faulty deduction, hypodermic shots in the main line on the spot — for a consideration.'

He passed a shaking hand along the side of his curling hair. His mouth opened but no sounds came from it.

'This young man Franklin is on your private list, isn't he?' I said.

'I have helped him, yes.' He let the words out as if they were being dragged from him by forceps.

'What's he hooked on?'

'Heroin.'

'How long?'

'Fairly recently, I believe.'

'How?'

'A fellow student was responsible.'

'His name?'

'You can't expect me to betray that, for heaven's sake.'

'Don't stall on me, Doctor. The name?'

'Bennion.'

'How did he come by *your* name?'

'From a man called Ellery, but look here . . . '

'How much are you shaking them down for?'

'They pay five pounds each visit.'

'Does it ever occur to you that a student will have considerable difficulty in raising that kind of money regularly?'

He moved his splendidly-tailored shoulders. 'That is no concern of mine.'

'The care of the sick is the concern of every doctor, isn't it?'

'Addicts are legally entitled to . . . '

'You make *me* sick, Doc. You're not giving them controlled treatment to get them off the hook. You're deliberately putting them on it — for money. I ought to shop you.'

He stood up again, trembling. 'You gave me your word, damn you!'

'I'm keeping it in this instance, exactly as I promised.'

'What do you mean — in this instance?'

'What I say. I'm not going to the police about John Franklin. But if you stay in this dirty racket I'm likely to have other thoughts. Putting it another way, I'm giving you time to quit.'

'You bloody Yank!' said Dr. Pascall thoughtfully.

'Very unprofessional language, Doctor, and it won't help you. I look forward to your immediate and exclusive resumption of general practice. Good day to you.'

I tramped out of his office, gave Miss Agnes M. Southey an obscene leer and went down to my car, suddenly remembering that I had omitted to lock the doors.

That was why Miss Paula Vincent was sitting in it.

10

She was in the passenger seat and reached across to nudge the nearside door open so that I could get into my own car. She was wearing a cool powder blue Italian two-piece over a white lambswool sweater and was sitting with her knees pressed together.

I slid down in the driving seat, turned the ignition key and listened to the engine purr lightly and tightly; they put some good machinery in this model.

'Where to, Miss Vincent?'

She bent a knuckle under her smooth chin and made a low, mellow laugh; almost a gurgle, which reminded me of Katie Allison, now married to more money than Shand is ever likely to see at close quarters.

'Is that all you've got to say?' she asked.

'No, but it'll do for a start.'

'I'm not going anywhere in particular,'

she said coolly. 'Just where you're going will do fine.'

'Humph!' I grunted and started driving, no idea where. We were out in the traffic and going east when I said: 'I'll give you lunch, if you like.'

'Very much, thank you kindly, good sir. Do you care for Italian food? You do — that's fine, too. I know a nice little place in Jermyn Street, if we can park close enough.'

'That disposes of one question, but not the second.'

'Which, of course, is how I come to be sitting in your car. Well, you forgot to lock it, for one thing.'

'How did you know it was mine?'

'It's my day off and I'd just been calling on a friend when I saw you drive up and go into that place. I thought I'd wait for you to come back.'

'Why?'

'I told you, it's my day off — I thought we might have a chat.'

'About what?'

'You *are* in an interrogative mood, aren't you?' She took out a white calfskin cigarette case and offered it.

'Not just now, I don't usually smoke when driving.'

'Sensible man. You don't really want somebody yack-yacking away in the passenger seat, either, if you're to concentrate.'

'I'll make out, Miss Vincent.'

'I shan't scream for help if you call me Paula. What's your first name?'

'Dale.'

'I thought that was a woman's name.'

'Both. I assure you, however, that my masculinity is beyond dispute.'

She gurgled again. Then she said: 'If you don't mind my asking, who were you calling on in that place?'

'A fellow named Pascall, a doctor.'

'Oh . . . ' She studied the end of her cigarette. 'I must say that rather surprises me.'

'You mean you know what he does there and I don't look like a junkie?'

'That more or less sums it up, yes.'

I didn't answer immediately. The driving mirror showed a big truck cutting out to pass at the penultimate moment with traffic coming towards us and I had to pull in to the left to let him do it, the stupid bastard.

'Confirming the opinion you've formed about me, I'm not on his hook or anybody else's, if it comes to that,' I resumed.

'I'm glad,' she said simply.

The traffic got worse, something I wouldn't have thought was possible, and I suspended conversation until we got to Jermyn Street. A dove-grey Aston Martin nosed out from the kerb, steered delicately by a tweedy fellow with a seamed aristocratic face who looked as if he was accustomed to the society of basset hounds, and I took over the tenancy.

We went into the little restaurant, ordered the *minestrone* as a starter, and instructed the wine waiter to unleash a bottle of Chianti.

'You half-tried to date me yesterday,' mused Paula. 'I'll bet you never thought you'd see me again.'

'I'd have got around to it,' I said. 'The thought was stirring in the back of my mind.'

'How frightfully flattering being at the back of your mind!'

'Tell me how you come to know about Dr. Pascall,' I said.

'Oh, that? It's common talk among some of the people who live nearby. Those who notice the comings and goings of all the weirdies, I mean.'

'Weirdies?'

'Well, not all weird. Some look like students. Some girls, too. It's a wonder the police haven't heard about it.'

The Chianti arrived and we touched glasses. When she put hers down she said: 'It's getting pretty bad, all this drug business. Especially among the kids.' She wrinkled her nose. 'The future parents of the nation — my God!'

'Plenty of swell kids around, though.'

'Nice to hear you say that, particularly . . . ' She smiled.

'Particularly as I'm not young.'

'Well, I didn't mean you're old.'

'Thanks.'

'Goodness, you're not touchy on that subject, are you?'

'No more than any other man coming

113

up to his fortieth anniversary. As to the younger generation, I think it's great — with exceptions which, though a minority, seem to be growing.'

'Yes, and bastards like Pascall ought to be behind bars. I hope you're not shocked by my candour?'

'No. In fact, you took the words right out of my mouth.'

The waiter brought the main course and we were halfway through it when she said: 'I don't want to pry, but you're something to do with the police, aren't you?'

'What makes you think that?'

'It was just an impression I got last night. Are you?'

'I'm a private eye, shamus or gumshoe.'

'Well, well! You don't look like some of the ones I've seen on TV.'

'I just look like me.'

'That's not a bad thing, Dale. By the way, that's the first time I've used your name, isn't it? Sounds nice and it fits you.'

'If my parents had christened me Clarence Murgatroyd it'd still have to fit me.'

She shook her head. 'There isn't any have to about it — a name either fits a personality or not.'

'Getting away from names,' I said, 'what do you know about Garfield Ellery?'

'The man you called on? Nothing — except that he's gone.'

I paused with a forkful of *cannaloni* in mid-air. 'When did this happen?'

'He went out last night, hasn't been back and isn't coming back. He left a letter with me for the manager, enclosing three months rent in lieu of notice.'

'I thought you finished at seven?'

'They asked me if I'd work on till ten, that's how I came to take the letter. He brought it to the counter. He didn't say what was in it, but the manager told me later.'

I put the *cannaloni* back on the plate, untasted.

Paula eyed me curiously and said: 'Has he done something . . . something illegal?'

For a long moment I sat there with my thoughts. I knew nothing about her except that she looked fetching and worked in the apartment block. She might be linked with Ellery in some way, for all I could tell; though somehow I couldn't believe it.

As if she were reading my mind she said quietly: 'You're debating whether to trust me, aren't you?'

I grinned. 'That thought was also stirring at the back of my mind — but I've just banished it.'

'Oh, why?'

I looked directly at her. Her eyes met mine candidly. They had the look of intelligence and, perhaps better still, of honesty. 'I don't think you have anything whatever to do with Ellery and I'm willing to wager money on it,' I said.

That's nice.' Then her long mouth pursed in distaste. 'I disliked him intensely,' she volunteered. 'He had a way of looking at me as if I had no clothes on.'

'I'd have thought you got a fair amount of that. Paula.'

She laughed. 'Well, yes, but it was the way he did it . . . something in his manner. I can't properly explain it, but it was . . . well, obscene.' She looked at her ringless hands, falling silent. I had a feeling that she was going to resume without prompting from me. After a moment she did. 'Shortly after you left — well, about half an hour or more later — someone came in and asked to see him. I . . . well, I thought I knew him.'

'How do you mean, you *thought* you knew him?'

'I saw his picture in a newspaper some time ago in connection with an armed raid on a bank security van — I'm certain it was the same man.'

'Who did you think he was, Paula?'

'The newspaper story described him as Harry Riceman.' Her mouth curled faintly. 'Handsome Harry Riceman were the exact words.'

I remembered the case. 'Riceman was charged with two other men but got off on an alibi plea the police couldn't break.'

Paula nodded. 'I turned up the case in the public library this morning — and the man who provided the alibi was Garfield Ellery.'

'You're sure?'

'Positive.' She looked at me and went

117

on: 'That's another reason I waited for you when I saw you leave your car. I wanted to find out what you thought.'

'Why me?'

'I've told you — I thought you were connected with the law in some way. I thought I could talk to you rather more easily than if I went to the nearest police station.' She hesitated, then put her long cool hand on mine, without speaking.

I made up my mind and told her pretty well everything. I thought: Carruthers will love me for this, like hell he will. But I had the intuitive feeling I've had times before, the certainty that you are with someone you can trust. Maybe events might prove that assessment wrong — but I was willing to lay odds against that, too.

'Well, my goodness,' Paula said when I had finished. 'Why, it's like being in a movie, only better.'

'And quite probably more dangerous.' I moved slightly and felt my knee touch hers. I got it straight back into quarantine and said: 'Did Ellery leave with Riceman?'

'Yes.' She hesitated and then said in a

rush: 'I overheard something he said to Riceman when he came up to the reception desk. I'll try to repeat the exact words. Now what were they? Oh, he said: 'We'll have to change plans after what's happened. We'll meet at Fenwick's Wharf at three tomorrow instead.' Then he said something about having told a man named Kessel-something-or other . . . '

'Kesselring.'

'Yes, that was the name. How did you know?'

I told her briefly and she added: 'Ellery also said: 'We'd all better take the cruiser over to the Continent, but we'll see how he reacts.' Those are the exact words, I think.'

It looked as if Ellery had got cold feet because of my involvement — but not cold enough to shy at an attempt to kill me. Enough to switch plans, though. Maybe Kesselring was made of tougher material? There was one way to find out.

I looked at my watch and said: 'Will you do something for me?'

'I think so.'

'I'm going to this place, Fenwick's

119

Wharf. I'll try to eavesdrop. I want you to go to Carruthers, the Intelligence man I told you about. He'll have to decide whether to move in or leave me to it.'

She looked at me earnestly. 'What you're going to do — it's dangerous, Dale. I don't like it.'

'I shan't show myself. Carruthers isn't ready to precipitate a showdown — he needs more information. This way I may be able to get some of it.'

'Why can't you simply leave it all to him?'

'I've pledged myself to co-operate, Paula. But that's not the sole reason. There's Amanda Chester . . . '

She made a small shiver. Then she said quite calmly: 'I'd rather come with you.'

'You'll do what you're told or else,' I growled.

'Or else what?'

'Never you mind.'

'I wouldn't mind anything from you,' she said.

'Meet me here at six-thirty and I'll take you up on that.'

'What — in a restaurant?' she asked

innocently. Then her face went serious again. 'You *will* be careful, won't you — promise?'

'Yeah.'

It was two o'clock when I left her and drove east beyond Tower Hill into the London the trippers know slightly and suburban commuters scarcely at all. A vast sprawling zone of narrow cobbled streets with stumpy posts and small shops and endless rows of houses clustered together for warmth and friendliness — and over everything the pervading imminence of the ship-crowded river and the docks and the great sweep of the Limehouse Reach and the Pool and, far down, the widening mouth where the two hundred and ten miles of river finally flows into the sea. The East End, where the accent is as sharp as the native wit.

Fenwick's Wharf was angled between the Limehouse Cut and Bow Creek about a couple of miles north of the Poplar Dock. I left my car on the last section of passable dirt road and walked, but not making a direct approach. The bank was steep and cluttered with rotted huts and abandoned warehouses. There was no one in sight and no sound closer than the distant stridency of a ship's siren far out on the broad river.

The bank was soggy with muddied grass and pools of watery clay; my new slip-on tan shoes were caked with it. I dodged round the decaying buildings, into lines of raggedy trees — anywhere that looked like cover.

Ten minutes, maybe a little more. Then I saw the place: a wood jetty and a discoloured boathouse, down below. Over the boathouse were the words *Fenwick's Wharf*. It didn't look much of a wharf, but this was it all right. I could clamber down the bank or come in from the rear. I took the latter route.

And only just in time. A motor hummed into life and in the next moment a cruiser thrust out from the jetty, going down the creek for the river. I flung myself flat on the bank, hands cupped to my eyes.

The cruiser went past, gathering speed but not making any high speed because the creek at this point was narrow and probably not deep. I caught a glimpse of an incredibly gross man with a silver grey crew cut. He was at the wheel with a cigar jutting from his thick sensuous lips. Then the boat was gone.

I looked at my strap-watch. Exactly three o'clock. They must have met earlier than Paula had heard. I was too late to get even the smallest chance of a clue, unless they'd left something behind in the boathouse, which seemed improbable.

It might be worth looking, just the same. Never leave anything to chance. I stood up and walked straight down to the place. There was no rear door, but now I didn't have to worry about taking cover. I went along the side, a narrow path which led to the jetty. Steps went down to the right, leading to the open doorway through which the cruiser had left.

Between the door and the creek itself was a basin contained at the other end by what looked like a small lock gate; but the gate hadn't been fully closed, so that the level of the water was rising steadily. That was why the skiff was rocking.

I stared down at it, with an eerie

sensation that something was wrong. Then the skiff suddenly jerked. I went down the steps and into the skiff and looked over the side.

A human hand was jutting above the water.

11

The hand was clenched and still twitching. I grabbed at it and hauled. Nothing happened. I could feel my back hair lifting. He was there — under the water, immovable. I kicked my shoes free, tore off my jacket and dived, swimming down.

He was standing erect with a ringed stone tied to his ankles, holding him for drowning. The stone was secured by cords. I got a pen-knife out of my pants pocket and slashed them. The body shot up like a cork erupting from a bottle, which meant that his lungs weren't yet flooded. But he was as near being unconscious as makes no difference.

I wound an arm round him and got him to the side; tumbling him into the skiff face down, wheezing and retching. The skiff was rocking madly. It was no place to do anything. I heaved his body sprawling on to the wood planks of the jetty and went to work on him, pumping the water out of his lungs. He was more than half-way to being dead, but now he wasn't going to die.

Finally, I had him propped up, his head sagging forward on his chest. His face was purpled with livid bruises and his underlip was split open. He was incapable of speech and likely to be for some time. What he needed was a hospital bed. I put my shoes and jacket back on and picked him up, a sobbing dead weight, and started back for my car. It seemed like a hundred miles away.

We were nearly there when a launch turned into the creek from the river. I stood on the bank with John Franklin still in my arms, yelling at the top of my voice.

The fellow at the wheel, a big man with the shoulders of a heavyweight boxer, saw me first and steered the police launch close in. A moment later he was on the bank.

'Sergeant Ballard, Thames Division, Metroplitan Police,' he said.

'Glad to know you, Sergeant. My name is Dale Shand. This man needs a doctor, quick.'

'Bring him on the launch, sir.' He led the way, adding over his shoulder: 'What happened — just saved him from drowning?'

'From murder by drowning.'

'So?' He said it phlegmatically.

I put Franklin down and a uniformed constable tried some additional first aid. Sergeant Ballard said: 'You weren't joking, I hope?'

'About murder? No, I was being quite serious.'

'I thought it might be suicide. We get several attempts every week — it's routine. But they're usually middle-aged spinsters and widows living in bed-sitters with the gas turned down. Lonely people who've given up the struggle. But this chap's only young. I suppose you don't know who he is?'

'Yes. His name is John Franklin and he's a third-year university student at St. Crispin's.'

'You know him well, eh — a friend?'

'No, I just happen to know who he is.'

The river patrol launch was making a wide arc and heading upstream, going fast. 'We're making for the Waterloo Pier,' Ballard said. 'While we're doing it you'd better explain, sir.'

I hesitated and he noticed it; he was a big stolid-looking man who would always notice more than a lot of people might give him credit for.

'If you think I'm being reluctant, Sergent, you'll not be wrong,' I said. 'But there chances to be a reason.'

'I think you'd better tell me, sir,' he said impassively.

'I went to Fenwick's Wharf. Just before I got there a cruiser nosed out and went down the creek towards the river. Then I saw a hand sticking out of the water in a basin at the wharf and I dived in. I found this boy with a paving stone tied to his ankles. I cut him free and managed to get him ashore.'

I glanced sideways to see how he was taking it; he appeared to be taking it with total imperturbability.

'And that's all?' he asked.

'No.'

'I didn't think it was, sir. What exactly were *you* doing there?'

128

'I can't go into detail, Sergeant.'

'I'm afraid you'll have to,' he answered bleakly. 'If your not prepared to make a full statement I shall have to hold you for further inquiries.'

I said: 'Look, everything is on the level. My reasons for being there are connected with an investigation being made by British security. I'll give you a name and a number to ring. The man you'll get through to is named George Carruthers. You can also check my standing with Detective Chief Superintendent Logan at Scotland Yard.'

'I'll do that, Mr. Shand,' he said. 'Meanwhile, I'll use the radio. Perhaps one or other of our launches can trace this cruiser you're talking about.'

We made Waterloo Pier, which is the only floating police station anywhere in Britain. They took Franklin in, called an ambulance crew and Ballard got on the telephone. He spoke briefly and listened at some length. Then he turned and said: 'They want to speak to you, Mr. Shand.'

I took the receiver from him. Carruthers said: 'Getting into trouble seems to be endemic with you, doesn't it?'

'Yeah.'

'Not your fault, though. Oh, I'll fix things with the Thames Division chaps. Any ideas?'

'About why they tried to kill young Franklin?'

'Naturally.'

'No firm ideas. A couple of theories that might fit, though. They could have judged him to be unstable because of his addiction and therefore expendable, or he could have become suspicious of their real aims and shown it.'

'It's possible. We'll have him questioned as soon as he recovers sufficiently. Anything else?'

'I saw a cruiser leaving the wharf, but if Ellery was in it he was keeping out of sight. I saw the guy at the wheel, though.'

'Describe him.'

'A very big guy, almost gross, with grey hair clipped to a crew cut. Smoking a cigar. He looked dangerous.'

'Kesselring,' said Carruthers. 'You say the cruiser was heading for the river?'

'Yes, the damned thing's probably

half-way to the Continent by now.' I told him what Paula had overheard.

'H'm, interesting,' was all he said.

'I thought you might throw the book at me for talking with her,' I remarked.

'I had that impulse for a moment, but on reflection no.' He made a small sound, like a chuckle. 'A highly presentable and intelligent young woman. We might be able to use her, if she's willing.'

'You seem willing to use anybody,' I grunted.

'From time to time, yes — but not anybody. By the way, she's still here. She appears to be somewhat anxious on your behalf. You must have made quite an impression there.'

'I'll join you in about an hour,' I said.

'Right.' He immediately hung up.

It was only then that I remembered I had left my car several miles downstream. Ballard said comfortably: 'We'll have you back there in quick-sticks in the launch.'

'I take it Carruthers explained the situation, Sergeant?'

'Enough to be going on with, Mr. Shand. You won't be held in durance vile, as they used to say.'

It was exactly fifty-nine minutes later when I walked into Carruthers' office, having paused on the way to put some dry clothes on. It occurred to me that I seemed to be handling the dampest assignment on record. Not a damp squib, though.

Paula jumped up from a leather armchair and gave me both her hands. 'I thought you were going to be careful,' she said rebukingly.

'I was, but the circumstances got somewhat out of my control.'

Carruthers grinned. 'When you know Shand a little better you'll come to expect the unexpected,' he said. He picked up a sheet of paper and went on concisely: 'A cruiser answering to the description you furnished is heading for the French coast due south of Calais. We've signalled Interpol with a request to investigate but not to do anything dramatic. They should be coming through any time now.'

'How about young Franklin?'

'He'll recover. Incidentally, he has about two dozen hypodermic punctures, intravenous injections. Heroin, apparently.'

'That must be how he got in with Ellery,' I said. 'But the man who introduced him to Pascall was a fellow-student named Bennion.'

'You haven't previously mentioned that name, my dear chap,' murmured Carruthers.

I grinned. 'I wasn't keeping something back for a lone wolf investigation. I simply haven't had time to report till now.' I went over the interview I had with Pascall.

Carruthers said: 'If he took the chance you gave him, he'll have left that place. Meanwhile, we have one murder and two attempted murders on our hands — or, rather, Logan has. It's his department and . . . ' Carruthers looked up as the door opened. 'Ah, on cue, as they say in the theatre. Anything?'

Logan took a chair without hurrying over it. He was a man who always conveyed the impression that he had all the time in the world at his disposal, which was deceptive — few police detectives I had known could think and move faster.

'This student, Franklin — he hasn't told us anything,' Logan announced.

'You mean he's still too ill?'

'He's ill all right. Half-drowned, beaten up, shock and suffering withdrawal symptoms until they gave him a mercy shot. But he's fully capable of talking, only he isn't.'

'You mean he won't?'

Logan nodded as he filled a blackened pipe. 'All we keep getting out of him is that he has nothing to say because he can't remember anything. The doctor says there is no trace of amnesia and no serious concussion.'

'Fear,' said Carruthers.

'Almost certainly. Bracewell, who is just about the best man on the strength at the interrogation, says all the signs suggest an almost panic fear of reprisals. Not without precedent unfortunately.'

'They left him drowning,' said Carruthers. 'A peculiarly sadistic touch, too. It fits what little we know of Kesselring. What do you think about it, Shand?'

'Just that we might put out a story to the newspapers that Franklin is suffering from total loss of memory and is unlikely to recover for months,' I said.

'Thus putting the enemy into a false state of security and quite possibly preventing a second attempt on Franklin's life?'

'Yes — except that their sense of security won't be false as long as Franklin refuses to talk. But I think we might do it.'

Logan said thoughtfully: 'We can't hold this young chap indefinitely. In fact, legally we can't hold him at all even on a drugs charge since he isn't actually in possession of heroin. He'll be free to go as soon as the hospital discharge him — unless he cares to discharge himself sooner. On the other hand, there's nothing to stop us putting a tail on him, as our Amercian friends would say.'

'I'll leave it to your judgement,' said Carruthers. 'Any clues about the dead girl?'

'Nothing so far. She wasn't seen by anyone in the flats the previous night.

Nobody saw her either going out or returning. So far as people there know, nothing happened. Incidentally, when Shand found her she had been dead since between eleven forty-five and one in the morning, approximately.'

Logan eyed me as if waiting for something. I said: 'She was killed because they thought she was associated with me. To that extent, I feel a personal responsibility for her death.'

'My dear Shand, you can't blame yourself,' remarked Carruthers.

'If I hadn't gone to Ellery's flat the chances are it wouldn't have happened.'

'You can't *know* that.'

'What other explanation is there?'

Paula, who had been sitting quietly looking from one to the other, leaned forward and touched my sleeve. 'Mr. Carruthers is right, Dale.'

I laughed without humour. 'It's swell of you all to say it, but I'll never rid myself of the feeling that I virtually signed her death warrant.'

Carruthers said levelly: 'I'm sorry about her death, it's a dreadful thing

— but we don't have room in this busines for sentiment. On the other hand, if that's how you feel you will all the more readily embrace the next stage of our activities.'

'And that is?'

'I'd like you to catch the next flight to Rome,' said Carruthers calmly.

'Not again! You got me there once before, a couple of years ago.'

'So you know the place, which is a small advantage. Bond will be delighted to see you again.'

'He didn't exactly give me three rousing cheers last time,' I said. I remembered him as a smart enough young agent if not quite so smart as his 007 namesake; I had managed to give him the slip and he hadn't been noticeably enthusiastic about it. 'What do you want me to do there?' I asked.

'Bond says that Horst Weidmann, the German student revolutionary leader, is in Rome. He is known to have some kind of affiliation with Kesselring.'

'That's interesting, but I don't quite see . . .'

'You will if you don't keep interrupting.

Bond says that Kesselring has an apartment near the Spanish Steps and that, before coming to England, most of his preliminary planning was done from there.'

'I get it. If Weidmann is in Rome he's probably going to meet Kesselring there.'

'You follow me like a leopard,' said Carruthers genially. 'Your immediate task will be to discover exactly what Kesselring is up to — and, if possible, the date when he expects to be back in England.'

'Why send me — can't Bond do it?'

'They both know him by sight. Neither Kesselring nor Weidmann has seen you.'

'Garfield Ellery has.'

'I omitted to mention it, but Logan's chaps say that Ellery is back in town. He probably wasn't even on that cruiser you saw. You will appear in Rome disguised as a holidaymaker.'

'Tourists are usually in parties or at least in pairs.'

'Yes . . . ' Carruthers said the word in a meditative way. Without moving in his chair he let his gaze dwell thoughtfully on Paula Vincent.

'For Pete's sake, you don't mean . . . ' I began.

Paula, who was sitting on the edge of her chair as if about to spring from it, said happily: 'I've just lost my job. I'd love to join in this.'

'Damn it, Carruthers,' I exploded, 'she doesn't know anything about the work.'

'So much the better, my dear chap. Miss Vincent won't have to *pretend* to be a tourist.'

'I won't let her do it!'

Paula said: 'Dale — I'm in this. If you won't take me I'll go it alone.'

'You can't *do* that . . . '

'Watch me, mate!'

Logan made a deep chuckle. 'You see, Shand — you're up against a highly determined young lady.'

'What guarantee is there of her safety?'

'You know better than to ask that,' observed Carruthers. 'There is no guarantee. Bond and two new men we have there will be on hand for anything you want. Beyond that — nothing.'

'I'm not asking for a guarantee Mr. Carruthers,' said Paula quietly.

He stood up behind his desk and said: 'You are a somewhat remarkable young woman, Miss Vincent. When you get back from Rome I'd like to discuss one or two things with you.'

'I'll be back,' said Paula.

Carruthers eyed me. 'Well, Shand?'

I waved both arms. 'I seem to be hoplessly outnumbered. If Miss Vincent is going into this anyway, she might as well tag along with me.'

'I absolutely love the enthusiastic way you put it, Dale,' murmured Paula.

* * *

An hour and a half later we were in the bar at Heathrow waiting for the flight to be called. Paula squeezed my arm and said: 'Don't look so angry, Dale — it's all going to be marvellous, I know it.'

I grinned at last. 'Why on earth did you take Carruthers up on this?'

'You shouldn't need to ask that.'

'Thank you.'

'Well, there *was* another reason. I mean if you had any idea how excruciatingly boring my recent life has been.'

'You surprise me.'

'Why?'

'Well, you're an uncommonly attractive girl. Offhand, I'd have said life ought to have been full of interest.'

'Full of wolves.'

'How do you know I'm not one?'

'I'm not quite sure whether you are or not, but even if you are I'm sure you're a sort of pedigree wolf.'

'Well, well!'

'A nice one, anyway.'

'That stuff about losing your job,' I said. 'You simply made it up, didn't you?'

'No I didn't. I decided it, which is a bit different, though I've phoned the manager and told him I'm going abroad and won't be coming back.'

'Suppose they sue you for not giving adequate notice?'

'He won't do that,' said Paula calmly. 'He works one or two fiddles which I happen to know about. Better still, he knows that I know.'

'Blackmail, eh?'

141

'It never fails,' said Paula. She looked at her watch and added: 'I've time to spend a penny. You have another drink and I'll be back in a couple of minutes.'

She slid off the high stool and was starting for the powder-room when a rangily-built fellow with a creased face which looked full of shabby cunning elbowed his way to the bar. His eyes, which were heavily hooded, flickered over me and went away. I had never seen him before, but I had an odd impression that he knew me.

I bought myself a small whisky and poured a little cold water in it. The newcomer, who seemed to be making a business of not seeing me, called loudly for the same.

The drinks came and he nursed his with both hands, then appeared to half-stumble.

'Sorry . . . ' As he spoke his right hand fluttered over my glass.

'That's all right,' I said.

'My foot caught in something. Lucky I didn't knock your drink flying.' He put his down and got a cigarette out.

I said: 'Do you happen to know the right time?'

He dropped his gaze to his watch and I switched the glasses round.

'Nine o'clock, or twenty-one hours airport time,' he said.

'Thanks. Bottoms up, then, eh?'

'That's right.'

We drank our drinks in unison. The shabby cunning on his face was replaced by scarcely-hidden delight.

'Great stuff, Scotch,' he said.

'In moderation, yes.'

'Dilates the arteries and stimulates the flow of blood, so the doctors say.'

'That's right. It helps to prevent a coronary thrombosis.'

'You might get something else, though,' he said with a grin which was only just removed from a leer of triumph.

Paula came back and I steered her away from the bar without speaking.

'What's the hurry . . . '

She didn't finish what she was saying because there was a heavy dull sound behind us and when I turned to look he was lying on the floor.

12

Before we reached the flight gate I tugged Paula's arm and said: 'We're not going.'

She started to gasp something but I was already going sideways with her across the departure lounge, not without small trouble because she was a strong girl and resistant. Fortunately, most of the people around were too busy making for their planes to notice.

'What on earth are you up to, Dale?' cried Paula.

'That guy who came up to the bar put a knock-out drop in my drink.'

'What!'

'Just before you came from the powder-room.'

'Then why aren't you lying on the floor?' she demanded.

'I didn't want to make a fuss, so I took the statesman-like course of changing the glasses round and now *he's* lying on the floor.'

'Oh . . . ' She made her small gurgling laugh, then she said: 'I still don't see why we can't go to Rome.'

'Think.'

She thought, wrinkling her nose. 'You mean that when he comes round he'll be on the phone to Kesselring and there'll be a reception committee waiting for us?'

I nodded. 'We'll go there — but not on this flight and not necessarily to Rome in the first instance. Meanwhile, I want to know about this guy — specifically, how he knew we were here.'

'Yes, that's a point. What do we do next?'

'Wait for him to recover and then find out where he goes.'

'He's seen you, hasn't he?'

'That can't be helped.'

'Yes it can. He hasn't seen me, not properly anyway. I'll tail him.'

I tugged her back again. 'You're not going off on your own, Paula.'

'Oh, yes, I am. There's no danger. I'll simply tell a taxi to keep him in sight.'

While I hesitated she said: 'It makes sense, Dale. I'll simply find out where he goes and come back to you.'

'All right. I'll get on to Carruthers and meet you at his office in an hour.'

'Good — and we'd better split up now before he sees us together. He won't be out for long, will he?'

'No, he'll be coming round shortly — feeling like death.'

'I'll take a seat in the lounge and wait for him, then. You just melt away.'

I went into a telephone booth and called Carruthers. He listened and then said urbanely: 'Quite a girl, our Miss Paula Vincent. I like her.'

'Humph,' I grunted.

'My dear Shand, you should be charmed at having so delightful a companion on your little adventure.'

'I don't want her hurt.'

'Nor I. But she'll be all right merely following this fellow in a taxi.'

'So long as she doesn't start having more ambitious ideas. What about Rome?'

'We'll have to see. I don't like the idea of Kesselring being ready for you.'

'I don't like the idea of anybody

146

knowing we were going there,' I said grimly.

'No, that's something we shall need to look into.'

'Is there a possibility of anyone having been planted in your department?'

'Everything is possible, Shand — though I find that particular possibility rather hard to credit. There must be another explanation.'

'I hope so,' I said and hung up. I took a concealed look into the lounge. Paula was no longer there. I walked out, as jumpy as a cat on a hot tin roof. Maybe I shouldn't have let her do it. I was already oppressed by the feeling that one girl had died at least partly because of me; I didn't want another. Also, I was starting to get fond of Paula.

There was no sign of her or the Mickey Finn man. They must have gone. I felt an irrational impulse for speed, as if that was going to help. I went outside the terminal building and hailed a taxi. 'Make it fast,' I said.

'Where to, guv?' the driver asked, not unreasonably.

I laughed. 'Sorry — Baker Street, near the Tube station. I'll give you the exact number when we get there.'

He meshed his gears and moved out of the rank. We were going down the Cromwell Road when I saw the two taxis ahead. The leading one made a left-hand turn. The brake lights of the second come on, then it made the same turn.

I leaned forward, rapped the glass partition and said: 'Follow those two cabs off to the left, driver.'

He didn't ask why. He merely said: 'Do you want me to pass them or not?'

'No, just keep a distance. I'll tell you what to do next.'

Three-quarters of the way down the street the first taxi stopped and the rangy man got out, or more accurately, tottered out. I caught a glimpse of his white, sick face before I ducked my own down out of vision.

He went across the pavement and down some steps into a basement which looked like some kind of storage place. Paula's taxi had gone on, to stop midway along the next block. I snapped at the

148

driver and we slid in behind it.

She was strolling back along the street when I got out, right in front of her.

'Well, well!' she said.

I paid off my driver and looked dourly at her. 'I thought you were merely going to find out where this guy went to,' I rumbled.

'That's precisely what I'm doing, darling.'

'Never mind the endearments . . . ' I began.

'Why, don't you like them?' she asked.

'Whether I like them or not has nothing to do with it.'

'All right, then — you asked me to find where he's going and that's what I'm doing.' She linked an arm in mine and went on cosily: 'I won't say it's not nice having you with me while we take a closer look.'

'But you'd have gone down into that damned basement on your own.'

'I might have. I was certainly going to risk a peep, anyway. Have you got a gun?'

'No.'

'I thought all American private eyes

went around rodded-up — that's the expression, isn't it?'

'You've been watching too much television. Anyway, private eyes, British or American, don't wear guns in this country. The police don't like it.'

'I thought you might have got a special dispensation, being sort of attached to the Secret Service.'

'As a matter of fact, I *have* got one, but I forgot to wear it this morning. Careless of me.'

'You might need one in Italy.'

'Bond, the agent out there, would fix us up. Well, me, anyway.'

'Me, too, I hope. I can handle one. My father taught me. Dad was an expert both with rifles and hand guns. We're here,' she added, stopping.

The basement was part of a shabby-looking kind of warehouse. Five worn stone steps led down to a cracked door whose last coat of green paint was probably put on around the time of the Munich Crisis.

We went down them soundlessly. At the bottom I poked an index finger at the door. It moved a little inwards. I wound my left hand round the tarnished brass knob and leaned my shoulder on the panels, using progressive pressure. The door went back without creaking. Maybe they kept the ancient hinges oiled?

'Stay right behind me and at first sign of any trouble run like hell,' I whispered.

We went in and down a short bare passage. There was another door at the other end. It was marginally open, enough to glimpse a section of the room beyond. Some kind of office. Cracked linoleum, a dark old-fashioned rolltop desk, open with a telephone on it. Mickey Finn was sitting on a swivel chair which he had pulled up to the desk and was talking down the telephone. He said what sounded like a swear-word, then:

' . . . I'm sorry, but the bastard changed the drinks round. All right, all right, I should've seen. He asked me the time and must've done it while I looked at my watch . . . '

A pause. His white face went tight. 'I couldn't help it, I tell you. Don't have me done up, Ellery . . . don't . . . ' He quit speaking, took the receiver from his ear and stared at it. When he put the phone down his hand was shaking slightly. He lurched off the chair, muttering to himself: 'I got to get out of this . . . I got to get out before they come for me . . . '

I closed a hand on Paula's and we went back into the street. She said: 'Why didn't you confront him?'

'Why waste time on a hireling?' I countered.

'I thought you'd feel like giving him a fourpenny one,' she said.

'He'll get more than that if he doesn't fade — and quickly.' I waved at a taxi and we got in.

Carruthers was waiting. He listened thoughtfully and then said: 'It establishes that Ellery was behind what happened at Heathrow, but it doesn't show how the devil he knew you were there.'

'Maybe I ought to have forced the fellow with the knock-out drops to talk.'

'No, you were right not to approach him. You might have got some results, but the price is one we don't want to pay. We're still not ready to close in on these people. Bringing Ellery in for a grilling wouldn't alter whatever plans Kesselring has. They'd simply carry on without him.'

'Meanwhile, what about Rome?' I asked.

Carruthers allowed his left eyebrow to lift fractionally. 'My dear chap, you simply proceed there.'

'Including me, I hope,' put in Paula.

'But of course. You board the flight leaving at three in the morning. There is, however, an important change. You will fly direct to Capodichino Airport in Naples. A self-drive car will be waiting at your disposal.'

'A diversionary move?'

'Yes. Ellery will contact Kesselring, but he will now have no knowledge of when you take off or, indeed, whether you are flying at all.'

'Somebody knew last time,' I said. 'Anything on that?'

'Nothing, I regret to say.'

'I suppose you've already interrogated all departmental staff — anybody who could, by any stretch of imagination, have knowledge of what was discussed in this room?'

'Precisely that.'

I thought back to the one-sided conversation we had heard in the basement off the Cromwell Road. Suddenly, I was aware that Carruthers was looking hard at me.

'Yes, Shand?' he asked.

I didn't answer immediately. Something had surfaced in my mind. A recalled fragment of speech. The man in the basement starting to say what sounded like 'Bugger off.' Suppose that hadn't been the word?

'You *have* thought of something,' murmured Carruthers.

'Yes — something the fellow with the drops said on the phone. It's just come back. I thought he was saying bugger off. What if he had been telling them to take the bug off?'

Logan, who had joined us, slapped a thigh with a ringing impact and stood up quickly. Carruthers, though less demonstrative, had a sudden look on his distinguished features.

Nobody spoke. Instead, we started going over every crevice of the room's furniture. You can plant sub-miniature microphones under desks, above doors, low down on skirting-boards — almost anywhere. Carruthers left his seat and crossed to the window. A small rifle-like gadget can fire a suction mike high up on a window where it can stay unnoticed. There wasn't one, though.

I went round to where Carruthers had sat and slid his desk drawers out. There were two on either side, one shallow and one deep, and a long drawer in the centre. I got this so far out that it almost fell to the carpet. I sent fingers exploring the base — and found it. A small combined self-powered transistorised microphone and tape recorder planted in the middle of the drawer and unless you pulled the drawer almost right off the runners it was virtually impossible to know the bug was there.

'Come over here,' I called.

Carruthers turned. 'You've found it?'

'Yes.' I detached the bugging device, laying it in the palm of a hand.

Carruthers said: 'Do you understand how this damned thing works, Shand?'

'I think so.' I put it on the desk. After a few moments I was able to start the playback . . . every word we had spoken came through clearly, though the reproduction wasn't perfect.

'There must have been another like this on the previous occasion,' I said.

'Attached to my personal desk,' snapped Carruthers. 'The bloody impudence of it!'

'Never mind the impudence — the thing is who could have access to your room?'

Angry forks spread upwards from the bridge of his nose. 'Practically anyone — from the cleaners to members of my staff.'

'We can probably acquit the cleaners. As to your staff, you've already screened them.'

'Yes, I'm positive. And yet . . . '

'Unless whoever planted this wore gloves there'll be fingerprints on it,' I said. 'You could match them against the dabs of every staffer who had an opportunity to get in here when your back was turned. I guess that means literally everybody.'

Logan said: 'I'll arrange that, if you want me to, George.'

'I don't like it, but we'll have to,' answered Carruthers.

'If they're innocent they have nothing to fear,' I said slowly. 'On the other hand, is it possible that anyone not connected with your adminstration could come in here?'

'I suppose it's possible. Not easy, but possible.'

'Have any visitors ever been in here, to your knowledge?'

'No, I'm quite sure about that.'

Logan grinned faintly. 'The only person who comes in here unannounced is the Minister himself. As a matter of fact, he looked in just before Shand was here on the last occasion.'

'Yes, I remember,' said Carruthers. 'Young Derek was with him.'

'Who's he?' I said. 'A staffer?'

'Good heavens, no. He's the Minister's son. He's at university and the old man was taking him out to lunch.' Carruthers eyed the bugging device grimly. 'I'll follow your suggestion, Shand,' he said, 'and if we match any prints up then, my God, there's going to be trouble for someone.'

★ ★ ★

Two hours later we were back at Heathrow. No more men with knock-out drops or any other kind of men who looked as if they even cared who we were or whether we were flying to Naples or Timbuktu.

We walked through the flight gate and out on to the tarmac and got on the big plane. Paula let a hand slide into mine.

'I'm glad we met, Dale,' she said.

'Because you're getting a free trip to sunny Italy?'

'Of course.'

'You've never been there before.'

'I've never been out of England before.'

'You'll love it.'

'I know I shall.' Without looking at me she went on: 'I'd love it just the same if we were going to Manchester or Wigan.'

'That's nice. But going anywhere with me is likely to be somewhat alarming at times.'

'Or exciting?'

'Both probably. Mind you, it may turn out to be totally devoid of any kind of excitement.'

'Then we'll have to make some ourselves,' murmured Paula.

13

The jet came in on time and we found the self-drive car waiting — one of the new front wheel drive Fiats, dark blue with a silver flash along the sides. We had been equipped with international and Italian licences and I turned to Paula and said: 'Want to drive?'

'Yes, I'd like to, though I'm not used to driving on the right.'

'Try. If you find it off-putting I can always take over.'

I had been here before and pointed out the way to the *Autostrada del Sole* which would lead us to Rome. Five minutes later I was lazing back in my seat looking at the scenery and savouring the aromatic warmth of Italy while she handled the car with the positive assurance of the born driver.

'How'm I doing, mate?' she said.

'I take back anything I've ever thought about women motorists.'

She laughed. 'Some women are bad drivers, but the idea that they're all bad is a bit of masculine vanity-boosting.'

'Plenty of lunatic men drivers.'

'There's a theory going round among the trick cyclists that to you men a car is a sort of release for aggressive male instincts and a substitute for frustrated sexual ambitions.'

'For God's sake,' I said, 'we're getting into deep waters, aren't we?'

'You don't regard a car in that way, then?'

'If I ever did I've outgrown it. Basically, a car is simply a means of getting from A to B — or even Z. I don't regard it as an extension of my personality.'

'Or your sex drives?' asked Paula innocently.

'I wish you'd give over, as they say up in Liverpool.'

'Liverpool — why, do you know it?'

'I had an interesting experience there some time ago.'

She wrinkled her nose. 'A girl, I suppose?'

'You can suppose anything you like.'

'I'm asking then.'

'Why?'

'Because I'm jealous of your past life.'

'It's been reasonably blameless.'

'What do you mean — *reasonably* blameless. There's nothing wrong in your having a girl. You're free.'

'I thought you were jealous.'

'So I am, I'm jealous about everything that happened before I met you. But that's another thing altogether.'

'Well, well! And I haven't even made a tentative pass at you yet.'

'No, you're a bit on the slow side, aren't you? I like that, though.'

'I can get into high gear every now and then.'

'I'll have to watch out for that,' she said. In the next second she was swinging the car over to the right of the nearside lane. 'It's as well I was watching *that*, too,' she added as an Alfa-Romeo screamed past with its wheels straddling both lanes. I caught a fleeting glimpse of a fellow with a dark tanned face crouched tensely over the steering wheel.

'You're doing swell, Paula.'

'Thanks. What was I saying?'

'You were considering what to do if I got into high emotional gear.'

'So I was.'

'You didn't say you *would* do.'

'You'll have to find that out for yourself,' answered Paula, looking straight up the *autostrada*.

We came to Rome. The city of soaring statues and wide *piazzas* under the blazing inexorable sunlight. The scorched grass of the Villa Borghese Gardens. The vast dome of St. Peter's A myriad honking motor horns stridently challenging a two thousand-year-old paganism standing almost cheek-by-jowl with the garish modernity of the Via Veneto.

'I want to see the Pantheon, the Forum and the Colosseum — and, of course, the shops,' Paula announced.

'You do that while I see Kesselring.'

'Heavens — I'd almost forgotten we were here on business. I'll come with you.'

'You won't, you know.'

'I'm supposed to be working with you, aren't I?' she demanded mutinously.

'You're just a cover girl for my real purpose,' I grinned.

We drove across the *Piazza Barberini*, turning into the Street of the Four Fountains and found the Albergo Americano. Bond was in the foyer — tall, slim and boyish, except in the eyes.

'Hello, Shand,' he said. 'Nice seeing you again.' He eyed Paula with frank admiration.

'Paula Vincent,' I said.

'Even nicer — that's a dreadful word, but it was meant in a complimentary sense.' Bond spoke rapidly in idiomatic Italian and a porter wrestled with our baggage. 'It's rather early for a drink, but I think this calls for one.' Without waiting for a reply he led the way into the bar. 'You always make the most admirable travel arrangements, Shand,' he said blandly.

Paula gave him a long cool look. 'Is that intended to convey something?'

'What will you have to drink?' Bond asked, ignoring the question. 'I recommend a *negroni*.'

'What's that?'

'Essentially an Italian concoction.'

'Coffee for me,' said Paula.

'As you prefer. We'll have *negronis*. I guarantee you'll like the stuff, Shand. Or perhaps you've had it before?'

'As a matter of fact, yes. Incidentally, your recent guarantee is about the only kind we're likely to get here.'

'Meaning exactly what?'

'Carruthers made it clear that there is no guarantee of our personal safety, though he stressed that you and a couple of other fellows will do your best to save us from extinction,' I said with a grin.

'We'll try. By the way, I deliberately refrained from meeting you at Naples — I might have been spotted.'

'Or tailed.'

'It's possible. But we're not being watched in here. I made quite sure of that before you arrived. This is one of the smaller hotels and none of Kesselring's chums ever come in.'

'Why, how many has he?'

'Several. Italian, German, French and a new fellow called Svendstrom who is an expatriate Swede. Nasty chap.' Bond sipped his drink and resumed: 'Rome is Kesselring's chief base and these fellows have been associated with him at various times.'

'I take it you know what Kesselring's plans are — or what Carruthers believes they are?'

'Oh, yes. Very ambitious, I must say. The biggest thing Kesselring has ever dreamed up?'

'The biggest thing anybody on earth has ever dreamed up,' I said. 'Who's going to pay him?'

'That, old boy, is what we want to know and is perhaps the central reason for your presence here. Kesselring doesn't know you from Adam, so you have a head start on the rest of us.' He lit a cigarette and added: 'Carruthers could have sent Fosdyke or Mannering, who are also unknown to Kesselring. The fact that he asked you is pretty damned flattering. You could do worse than join us permanently.'

'I can do better not joining you as a staffer.'

'Probably, but you'd have security, the possibility of rapid promotion and a pension to match your retiring status.'

'I've never considered being pensioned-off by anybody,' I said. 'Maybe I should start considering it soon.'

'Good God, listen to him — you'd think he was pushing seventy,' said Paula.

'Would you?' asked Bond gravely.

'Not really.'

Bond's face stayed inscrutable; but, then, there was nothing to make it scrutable. He couldn't know that, though. He said: 'Just how are you going to tackle this, Shand?'

'I'm a renegade C.I.A. agent now working for an American underground group operating in several fields and having links with the international student revolutionary movement.'

'You'll need something that looks like proof,' Bond said.

'Carruthers fixed me up with names and some reasonably convincing background credentials. They won't stand up to intensive probing, but they should be enough to get me through the front door.'

'And out again, I hope,' remarked Paula seriously.

'What names are you going to drop, Shand?'

'Lance Bayard, Frank Auberlin and Jesse Nolan. All known sympathisers with Cuba and Hanoi and currently infiltrating into student protest in the States. Kesselring is thought to be planning contact with them, but so far they're only names to him — which is why Carruthers picked them.'

'It should be adequate,' Bond conceded. 'When are you going to put it to the test?'

'Today.'

'And Miss Vincent?'

'She stays behind.'

'What's the point in my being here if I don't do something?' Paula argued.

'I told you — if by any chance our arrival has been noticed your presence will have lent colour to the idea that we're a couple of tourists.'

Bond smiled. 'I can take Miss Vincent on a sightseeing tour,' he mused.

'Except that Kesselring knows you by sight,' I said.

He sighed. 'Yes — that's a pity.' He

glanced towards the door as two men came in. 'They're harmless,' he reported.

After a while he left and we passed a good deal of time seeing what there is to see in Rome, or some of it. You really need around three weeks. I finally left Paula to browse among the elegant *boutiques*, arranging to meet in a couple of hours.

'Take care, Dale,' she said quietly.

'I'll try.'

'Do more than that . . . I want you back . . . '

I drove through the zany Roman traffic, parked near the fountain opposite the Spanish Steps and found the Via Fabia. Number sixteen was a private entrance apartment at street level in a terra cotta block with blue and white striped awnings over brass-studded doors. A recessed bell-push played a couple of mellow bars, very *pianissimo*, footsteps sounded, the heavy door opened and I was looking at Kesselring. Close up, he loomed even larger than when I had seen him in the cruiser.

He was probably in his early fifties and

certainly in the region of forty pounds overweight without the blue mohair suit and the custom-made black Oxfords on surprisingly slim feet. He was also illegally wearing a Grenadier Guards tie whose knot was concealed by one of three chins in a face curiously devoid of colour. A gross, flabby and utterly expressionless face, but the eyes didn't suggest any kind of mental flabbiness; they were a very chilled blue and hard as diamonds, if less attractive.

Before he could say anything I spoke in English: 'Mr. Kesselring?'

'Yes.' The voice was deep and faintly guttural, but not heavily Teutonic — a sort of schooled vocal anonymity.

'My name is Peterson, Charles Peterson. I'd appreciate the opportunity of talking with you on a matter of mutual interest.'

'Oh? I don't believe I know you, Mr. Peterson, and I don't know that we have anything to discuss together.'

I smiled. 'I should explain that I am not unknown to a certain group in America whose aims may not be dissimilar to

170

yours, Mr. Kesselring.'

'I haven't the smallest idea of what you imagine yourself to be talking about,' he said.

'The group I am referring to is headed by Bayard, Auberlin and Nolan. Does that help?'

He shrugged his enormous shoulders. 'I am still quite in the dark,' he said. Then he made a tactical slip. 'If, however, you think it useful I can give you ten minutes, Mr. Peterson.'

We went across a small square hall and into a lounge full of dazzling sunlight and manufactured antique furniture.

'You are fortunate to find me in,' Kesselring remarked. He smiled without meaning. 'Incidentally, how did you know where I live in Roma?'

'Lance Bayard told me you were living here at least part of the year and suggested that I might look you up. He wasn't completely sure of the street address, but I located it.'

'Interesting — and perhaps a little surprising, since I am quite unacquainted with anyone of his name.'

'Well, he doesn't claim to know you personally, Mr. Kesselring. He knows of your work and feels that you may be interested in an association with our own work in the States.'

'Indeed?' Kesselring's vast face was still about as animated as cold suet pudding. 'I have yet to ascertain the nature of this work you persisted in talking about.'

'Suppose we quit being coy with each other, Mr. Kesselring?'

He took out a gold cigarette case, extracted from it a flat brown cigarette with a gold tip and lit it with a gold lighter, exhaling a long slow stream of Turkish smoke. 'I think perhaps you had better explain that last remark, Mr. Peterson,' he said gently.

'Let's say there is a small but resolute group in the U.S. opposed to existing military and political objectives and also working in the sphere of organised student revolt — or, specifically, such wrecking sectors of it as are ready for infiltration from outside the campus. How does that appeal to you?'

The gross man took the cigarette

from between his thick lips and said distinctly: 'It doesn't, Mr. Peterson. I am engaged in international finance, not international subversion, commuting between Rome, Zürich, Paris and London. I have not the slightest conception of or interest in what you are talking about.'

'Then I and my associates have been misinformed.'

'I will put it another way, Mr. Peterson. Not only am I not even remotely interested in political movements designed to destroy an economic system which has at all times been both congenial and lucrative to me, I am implacably opposed to them.' He smiled with his mouth but not with his zero eyes and added: 'I must assume that your friends have confused me with some other person and it therefore follows that you are wasting your time as well as my own. In short, you have come to the wrong man.'

'Then I owe you an apology, Mr. Kesselring.' I looked directly at him and said: 'Perhaps there *has* been a confusion of names. I'll have to try the others they gave me.'

A small flicker came and went in his eyes. Very fast. But he didn't make the tactical error of asking me.

'The man in London my group wish me to contact is named Ellery — Garfield Ellery,' I said.

'And you suppose that this is of interest to me, Mr. Peterson?'

'I don't know. Is it?'

'Not in the slightest.' He strode across the big room, doing it with the kind of easy lightness some big men seem to achieve. 'Would you care for a drink before you go?'

'No, thanks.'

'As you wish. I shall take a little *cognac*.' He poured rather more than a little and stood there with a sausage-like hand engulfing the blown-out goblet. After a moment he resumed thoughtfully: 'I am most sorry that you have had a fruitless visit — though you have not come to Rome solely to see me, I take it?'

'No, I happened to be coming over anyway. As I've explained, your name was suggested to me as a possible contact.'

'Among others, eh?'

'That is so, Mr. Kesselring.'

He sipped brandy and said: 'If you will permit the observation, you do not look like the kind of man who would be involved in anything so naïve as student revolt.'

'It's only a part of activities covering a rather more meaningful field of operations.'

'Indeed? Then as a supporter of political and economic orthodoxy I ought perhaps to inform the authorities.' A fat chuckle escaped him. 'Why, I could no doubt have you arrested, Mr. Peterson.' There was a small sardonic inflexion in the way he pronounced the name.

'I doubt it,' I said. 'For one thing, my credentials are impeccable — and I should, of course, deny any report you cared to make of this conversation.'

He promoted the chuckle into a laugh, which he seemed able to do without opening his mouth. 'You are a practised exponent of stout denial, eh?'

'There are few men who can excel me

in that exercise, Mr. Kesselring.'

'Admirable! Though there could, of course, be circumstances in which even the stoutest denial might disintegrate,' he said obliquely.

'Perhaps . . . ' I stopped as the sound of movement came from somewhere in the apartment.

'Excuse me one moment, Mr. Peterson.' Kesselring went out of the room. He was back inside a minute. 'My chauffeur,' he said apologetically. 'I had arranged for him to drive me.'

'In that case I will bid you *buona sera*, Mr. Kesselring.'

He shrugged. 'There is no immediate hurry. Not for ten minutes. You are sure you will not join me in a drink?'

'Thanks again, but no.'

Kesselring eyed me thoughtfully and said: 'You interest me, Mr. Peterson. You have the look of an exceptionally level-headed man. I still find it difficult to see you in the context of this underground revolutionary nonsense.'

'That could apply to a number of men answering to the same description.'

'The organising brains who manufacture or stimulate such movements for their own purposes, eh?'

'You could say that.'

'And you are one of their number?'

I gave him back his recent look. 'I thought I had made that reasonably clear.'

'To the meanest intelligence?'

'I wouldn't place your own intelligence in that category, Mr. Kesselring.'

He waved a ringed hand. 'The tribute is appreciated, but I prefer to deploy my intelligence in less dubious ways. How long are you planning to stay in Italy?'

'Not long.'

'You are off to London to see this other man — what did you say his name was?'

'Garfield Ellery.'

He shrugged, a fine shrug conveying total lack of interest. 'It is a pity that a man of your stature should waste his talents playing at tinpot revolution. There can be little in it financially.'

I said nothing.

Kesselring finished his drink, put the glass down and said: 'In the western world the established order will remain intact, you know. I now bid you good day.'

He strode buoyantly to the door and held it open, almost bowing me out. There was no sign of another car either on the forecourt or on the quiet, tree-lined street. I had a vaguely uneasy feeling. I had achieved nothing, learned nothing. Better go back to the hotel, for the time being at least.

Paula wasn't in the bar or the lounge. I ran upstairs. The door to her room was open and I went in. She wasn't there. Suddenly, I was sweating and not solely because of the climate.

I found the *concierge* and almost shouted: 'Has the Signorina Vincent gone out?'

'*Si*, mebbe ten minutes ago or a little more. Someone call for her. A *signor* in a car.'

'A man in a car — who?'

The *concierge* waved helplessly. 'I do not know, Mr. Shand.'

'What sort of man?'

'A small *signor* with a dark face

— much sun, you onnerstan'. He arrive in an Alfa-Romeo and ask for the English *signorina*, not by name.'

A dark-skinned man in an Alfa-Romeo. It fitted the man who had swept past us on the *autostrada* from Naples. Paula had seen the car . . . but perhaps not the dark, tanned face?

'Do you know where they went?'

'I regret no, *signor*.' He looked at me anxiously. 'Is there something not so good?'

'There's something bloody wrong,' I said.

I drove back to the Villa Fabia. I might still be in time, though I doubted it, but I had to try. I remembered Kesselring going out of the room and talking to the man he said was his chauffeur. That must have been when he fixed it; that was why there was no sign of another car when I went back for mine. He had sent for her and kept me talking long enough for the chauffeur to decoy her out of the hotel. And I had fallen for it. Shand the great detective. I recalled the faintly sardonic way Kesselring had pronounced the phony name I had given him. He had known all the time who I was.

I parked outside the apartment and went up the steps. The door was locked and nobody answered the ring. I manipulated the wards, but it was bolted on the inside. There was a partly open window down the side and I got in that way, into a kitchen with a door to the hallway. Five minutes later I had covered every inch of the place.

Kesselring had gone. Everybody had gone. And Paula with them . . .

The phone rang. I picked up the receiver and his fat voice purred. '*Mr. Peterson?*' The sardonic emphasis was explicit now.

'Shand,' I said.

'But, of course. I thought you would return to my apartment the instant you discovered your — shall we say bereavement?' A chuckle, then: 'However, you will be relieved to know that Miss Vincent is in good health . . . for the moment.'

'I'll kill you, Kesselring,' I said.

'Now you are being melodramatic and, worse, unrealistic, Mr. Shand — since you have no means of knowing where I am. We, on the other hand, know exactly where you are located. You will remain in your hotel until I contact you with precise instructions. That will be when we have reached our next destination. You will not have to wait long — though no doubt it will seem long, eh?'

'Let Miss Vincent go — it's me you want, Kesselring.'

'You are wrong — and, in any case, pray do not bandy words with me, Mr. Shand. It is also much better that you do not make any ill-judged move. You will hear from me in — let us say three hours. *Arrivederci* . . . '

I started to say something, anything. But the line went dead.

14

I could get hold of Bond. I could go to the police. I could raise a hue and cry. But I knew I could do none of these things. Kesselring had made certain of it by the simple move of abducting Paula. One false step and they would kill her.

God Almighty — what a mess you've made of it, Shand. Maybe you're batting out of your league, chum? No, that wasn't true. I had been in combat with at least two men no less dangerous and astute than Kesselring. But this time I had goofed somewhere along the line. I couldn't have known that the overtaking Alfa-Romeo was being driven by one of his mob ... but I could have warned Paula to ignore any message or any approach, to accept nothing that hadn't come from me in person.

Well, I hadn't done it and now they'd got her and I daren't even contemplate the risk of going to Bond or anyone else.

Kesselring couldn't have made more sure of my silence if I had been struck dumb. All I could do was go back to the hotel and sit there sweating, waiting for him to come through on the telephone with his orders.

And then? The answer to that was as clear as the Roman sky. He would tell me what to do and where to go and the place would be the slaughterhouse.

I looked at my watch. It said seven forty-five. Only minutes since he had phoned. I still had nearly three hours before he rang again. What the hell difference did that make?

Three hours. That gave him time to drive a hundred miles. A hundred miles in any direction. Heading north on the *autostrada* for Milan. Going south for Naples. Eastbound for the long flat Adriatic shoreline. Anywhere. He must have broken the journey somewhere to phone me and . . . I stopped as another thought started. Suppose he was already at what he called his next destination? It didn't *have* to be hundred miles away.

I yanked the receiver off its rest and got

through to the operator. A girl. She could speak English and was delighted to use it on someone. It wasn't difficult to explain what I wanted, though it took her a little time to get the information.

Then I had it.

'The last call to the number from which you speak, sir, was made through the operator at Ostia. The caller was speaking to you from Ostia 67085.

'*Grazie, signorina.*'

She laughed. 'Your accent is not so good, sir. Also, I prefer to hear you speaking English.'

I said: 'The Ostia number — can you also tell me the address?'

'I am most sorry, but it is not permitted to disclose this information, sir.'

'Not even for a friend who speaks English?'

'Alas, no, but . . . ' She lowered her voice to a conspiratorial huskiness. 'But if you examine the telephone book you may find the answer on Page 1011.'

'*Signorina*, you are most kind and, I am sure, most beautiful.' I hung up, riffled through the directory and matched the number with the address within seconds. The Villa Bella, via Messina. The beautiful villa. Like hell it was beautiful.

I went out to my hired car and drove fast, up to the frontiers of recklessness, like any good Italian. Ostia — a dozen miles west of the city, the seashore resort packed every week-end by perspiring Romans fleeing from the urban heat of high summer. The blue Mediterranean, white sands and bronzed bodies lazing in the sun by day and drinking in the open-air cafés by night. Kesselring wouldn't be among them; he would be holed-up at the beautiful villa savouring the thought of Shand sweating it out in the Albergo Americano.

Twelve miles in seventeen minutes concentrated driving. Then down into the slow twenties, finally crusing to a stop on the crowded front, a couple of yards from a short-sleeved traffic cop who told me how to find the via Messina.

I parked under a garlanded lamp standard just short of the mouth of the street and walked. The villa was at the far end, rising from a sandstone promontory which sloped in terraced undulations to the serene waters of the Mediterranean curling over shining black rocks.

There were lights in the place, though not from all the rooms. A dove-grey Maserati stood on the shingled drive alongside the Alfa-Romeo. I didn't go in that way. I walked just beyond the house, then moved at an angle through a cluster of mixed orange and lemon trees which formed part of a small orchard. I went under the scented branches. At the point where they ended I could see, to my right, a flat lawn in the centre of which was a swimming-pool with a black-and-white tiled walk-round, an ornamental fountain showing two small boys in the simulated act of urination, and a line of royal blue changing cabins.

I thought I heard a small swishing sound from the pool, but when I glanced across no one was swimming. I didn't go close because I would have been silhouetted in the moonlight; instead, I kept to the line of the villa at the rear, almost flattened against the ochre-coloured wall and moving slowly, testing each footfall.

Suddenly, light blazed from a ground-floor window which spanned most of the villa's width. I stopped dead in my tracks, listening to the small thunder of my heart, but nobody pelted out brandishing revolvers. All that had happened was that someone had switched the lights in in the room behind the vast window.

I couldn't risk peering in. I went backwards, round the corner of the place and some distance down the side. There was no light here. I used the fingers of both hands to explore the surface of the wall and found a door. It had a trigger handle. I depressed it slowly. There was the smallest click and the door opened inwards. I had a gun Bond had given me, a .32 Smith and Wesson automatic with a ribbed rubber grip, but no torch — not that it would have seemed a good idea to use one. I stepped inside the door and stood still, waiting for my vision to adjust itself.

Finally, I could see just enough of the way ahead. I was in a small room apparently used for miscellaneous storage. I dodged between old cabin trunks and a giant-sized vacuum cleaner and found my way into another room. Objects swam dimly into view — a desk, a padded leather chair, filing cabinets. I stepped very lightly on to the tiled floor — in this climate they don't use carpets.

The third door and light seeped under it. I had no way of knowing what was on the other side. Kesselring, Bowles and Lapete sitting in a semi-circle with sawn-off shotguns aiming? It seemed improbable — and, anyway, I couldn't stand in the dark all night. But I could listen. Nothing. Then, quite suddenly, the sound of voices — distantly, coming from a room beyond the one immediately in front of me.

I pushed at the door, watching it swing inwards without sound. It wasn't another room; it was a square hall with a mosaic floor, Moorish in pattern like the floors you can see in the Sicilian homes of the rich, clinging to their feudal overlordship with the Mafia everywhere.

The voices became clearer. Kesselring's detached itself.

'In perhaps another hour we will give

Shand his instructions . . . he should then be in an interesting state of apprehension.'

An American voice next. The accent was Las Angeles. 'Suppose he doesn't play along?'

'My dear Bowles, he has no choice,' answered Kesselring.

'You mean on account of the broad?'

'The young lady? But of course. Our good friend will inevitably be most disturbed by her plight.'

I crossed another yard of mosaic, up to the last door. Somebody spoke in Italian. Kesselring said: 'We will use English here, Belligi — all the time we are in your native country we will use it. And do not doubt that Shand will obey our orders — he must.'

'You think thees man will simply walk into the trap?'

'I think he will come to the villa, Tony. It is possible that he will try to get in unobserved. But for that we shall be ready.'

There was a small scraping sound, like a match being flared. Then Bowles was talking again. 'Shand — I heard about him back in L.A. I tell you this guy is trouble.'

'I do not need you to inform me of that, my friend, I am fully aware of it.'

'Yeah? He's also dangerous.'

'He will not be much longer.'

Bowles said viciously: 'I'll give it to him the first second he shows.'

'Not quite so fast as that, Al.'

'Why not? We want this guy dead, is all.'

'He will die, most assuredly — but not before we have a little conversation. You think there is a risk? What possible risk can there be once Shand is in our power?'

'This fellow has a reputation for getting out of tight corners. I say we don't give him even the ghost of a chance.'

'You are allowing yourself to become rattled, my friend. I have plans for Mr. Shand — and, indeed, for the beautiful Miss Vincent.'

The Italian made a sound, not pleasant. 'Let me have her, *signor* . . . '

'To wreak your will on, eh? It may yet be arranged, *amico*.'

A new voice said something in an alien tongue. It sounded like Swedish. That meant Svendstrom was there, making the known odds four-to-one. It might be even more.

But at least I was going to have the advantage of surprise. I held the automatic down my thigh with the safety-catch off and spread the palm of my free hand against the panelling. The door opened inwards, but I didn't follow through. The voices had stopped, as suddenly as if they had been turned off by a tap. Something was wrong.

There was a small fast movement in the room, then silence again. I stepped sideways, but no one came through the door. Then I heard the sound — almost directly behind me. I wheeled completely round, very fast but not quite fast enough because he was standing right in the centre of the hallway and I was looking down the muzzle of a model 1200 Winchester pump-action shotgun. With one of those things you can blow a brick wall wide open.

It was being held by a roly-poly man in

a shiny blue serge suit and a wide-brimmed straw hat jammed on a bullet head. Above the flag ears no hair grew, but the moon-like face was sprinkled with countless tiny silvered bristles, as if he hadn't shaved recently.

'To paraphrase a historical quotation — Meester Shand, I presume?' he said. It was the thick alien voice I had heard from inside the room.

Kesselring strolled through the doorway, beaming. 'There is another exit from this room. It enabled our good friend Svendstrom to take you from the rear.' He enlarged his smile. 'So you save me the small trouble of telephoning you in Rome, eh? Most thoughtful.'

He almost danced up to me. There was a blur of motion as his hand whipped my face side to side. He danced back, then came in again with a jab which nearly bent me double in agonising nausea. The gun I had, clattered to the tiled floor.

'Use the pump on him, Svend,' Bowles whispered. 'I want to see this bastard come apart.'

Kesselring chuckled. 'Not till I say.' He

reached out a hand and yanked my head upwards by the hair. 'He will come apart, Al — but not just yet. We have done enough for the moment. Now we have the little talk, most cosy. In the room, eh?'

Tony Belligi kicked me behind the left knee, expertly. New pain speared through me. 'Inside, *signor*.' He grinned wolfishly. I recognised him as the one who had passed us on the motorway.

I almost lurched through the door into a room about thirty feet by twenty. Belligi slammed me down in a deep hide leather chair.

Kesselring poured brandy. He sipped some of it and said meditatively: 'You look like a man sorely in need of a drink, Mr. Shand. Be my guest . . . ' He flung the rest of the spirit in my face.

I sat there with a primitive compulsion to murder while he resumed: 'You must tell us how you come to be here so soon — and, more particularly, how you discovered *where* to come, Mr. Shand.'

I still said nothing. Kesselring beamed again. 'Do not exasperate us, Mr. Shand. We have methods of persuasion. In the last global war I myself was an eager young apprentice with the Gestapo here in Rome. I invariably found that the reluctance of the interrogated collapsed under the appropriate pressures.'

If he thought I was scared he wasn't wrong. Any man facing torture is scared, like any soldier in the penultimate moment before combat. Courage doesn't consist in not being afraid but in fighting on despite the fear. But this wasn't the time to fight. Maybe there wasn't going to be a time.

'You were about to tell us how you found our little retreat, Mr. Shand . . . '

'You made a mistake,' I croaked.

A small reflex pulsed on his bull neck. 'I never make mistakes,' he said.

'You called your apartment knowing I'd go straight back there when I found Miss Vincent was missing. You couldn't resist the impulse to taunt me over the telephone. So all I had to do was get through to the operator and trace the source of the call. It was as simple as that — and you made it possible.'

Kesselring's face was a silent snarl. He

banished the look and said: 'Ve-ry adroit — but as you have gained nothing, it follows that you are less smart than you think.'

'Why all the elaborate scheming?' I said. 'You could have tried to deal with me when I first went to your apartment.'

'You are still the fool who thinks he is the clever one. It was necessary to disarm not only yourself but your pretty partner, and it amused me to arrange for her abduction — knowing that I could then call whatever tune I desired.'

'Only it didn't go exactly as you planned, Kesselring.'

'Not completely — but nearly so. You overlooked the fact that there we take many precautions, not least by ensuring that the lightest touch on the door to this room activates an alarm signal light on the inside.'

Svendstrom said: 'Joost the same, he knew something because he started to move from the door.'

'You all stopped talking too suddenly,' I sneered.

'We must watch that another time,'

mused Kesselring.

I stared round the room. Kesselring said: 'You are wondering where the luscious Miss Paula Vincent is, eh? Have no fear, she has not yet come to any harm. I cannot, of course guarantee this indefinitely . . . indeed, I cannot guarantee it more than a little while.'

'You've got me,' I said harshly. 'Isn't that enough?'

'Unfortunately, no. Miss Vincent also knows too much.' Kesselring poured himself another brandy, leaned forward and went on: 'You will now relate exactly what you both know of our organisation.'

'And if I refuse?'

'We have a deep cellar . . . your screams will go unheard,' Kesselring purred.

I cringed in the chair and whined: 'I'm willing to talk. I'm in this professionally, but they're not paying me enough to die — by inches or any other way.'

Kesselring said contemptuously: 'Al, I thought you told me this man has a tough reputation.'

'He has.'

'Then it is based on sand. Observe

— he is almost abjectly eager to talk.'

'It's out of character . . . '

'How do *you* know?'

'Okay, so I don't, not personal. But that's how they figure him back home.'

'On what grounds?'

'This guy put the finger on The Organisation — the way I got the picture he smashed it almost single-handed.'

'I still say you have been misinformed,' grated Kesselring.

Al Bowles shrugged. A door at the side of the room opened and a man in white slacks and a blue fisherman's jersey came through it. A man with a sallow face, darting black eyes and a quiff of black hair. I guessed he was Lapete.

Kesselring said impatiently: 'Tell us how you come to be interested in our work, Mr. Shand.'

'A girl named Amanda Chester asked me to check out some activities of her boy friend, a student called John Franklin. That led me to Garfield Ellery. Then British Intelligence asked me to widen the inquiry into a group believed to be exploiting a student minority. That led me to you.'

The gross man laughed. 'And you think I shall be satisfied with that as an explanation?'

'No, I don't think that. I was giving you a bald outline. Intelligence say you go in for political assassination — at a price.'

Kesselring laughed again. 'Ah — now we approach more closely to the truth. But why should I waste time listening to your garbled knowledge?'

Belligi said: 'I get thees man to make the confess in the detail, *si*?'

Kesselring stood up toweringly. 'Who now cares what the stupid Shand has to say? I weary of his words. I will tell *him* . . . '

Lapete spoke for the first time. He had a curiously high-pitched voice, almost soprano like a boy chorister. There was no other point of resemblance. 'Is it wise, *m'sieu*?'

'To let Shand into our little secrets? Why not — since he will never be able to repeat them? At least, not in this world.

What he reports in the next one is of no moment.'

'I'd have supposed you were too big to dissipate your talents on militant students,' I jeered.

'Students!' He almost spat out the word. 'What are they but *canaille*?'

'Nevertheless, you're using them — or some of them.'

'They have their place in our grand design. To that extent they are necessary.'

'But the real purpose is something bigger?'

'Shall I say that we have perfected the details of a coup without precedent both in scope and reward?'

'Assassination is the operative word, isn't it?'

An odd look came on his face and went away almost immediately. Then a grin split his thick mouth. 'So . . . so the bungling British Intelligence send Shand the shamus out on their behalf to take the risks they are unready to embrace. They will not, I fear, get much value for whatever fee they are paying you. Not that you will collect it.' Without change of

199

tone he added: 'Bring the girl in!'

It was Tony Belligi who went for her. I wanted to feel my knuckles smash his eagled nose, but I couldn't move from where I was and live. If I was going to live much longer.

He came back within a minute, forcing one of her arms up her back. His free hand slid lingeringly down her thighs.

'Dale . . . ' She tried to come towards me. Belligi put out a foot so that she pitched to the floor. She scrambled up and ran to me. I held her, saying nothing. There wasn't anything to say.

Kesselring lit a cigar, poking it in a match flame, then carefully blowing the flame out. 'In my leisure moments I have a most interesting hobby,' he said. 'You may like to hear something about it.' The voice was soft, but inside me something froze.

'Fishing is my pastime, Mr. Shand,' he resumed. 'Fishing on the grand scale, for I am not one to be satisfied with anything less.' He blew a perfect smoke ring and watched it with delight. Then he said gently: 'Come — I show you!'

We stood up together. I wondered whether to try something, but it still wasn't the time. It seemed improbable that there was going to be a time, ever.

Kesselring threw open the centre section of the huge french window and stepped through the doorway into the night. The others hemmed us in, like a bodyguard. Over his shoulder, he called: 'I have fished in many waters, but I prefer the warmer seas, not least the immense deeps of the South Atlantic. Waters alive with shoals of little tunny-like benito, the brilliantly-hued dolphins, cruising schools of octopus and squid . . . but, above all, the real giants against which to pit comparable strength.'

I had a nightmare presentiment of what was coming. Paula's hand, cold and damp, gripped mine.

Kesselring let more words flow, mingling with the aromatic cigar smoke. 'I have even caught with rod and line that freak of the ocean, the hammerhead shark . . . but it is another of the same family I most especially like.' He stepped sideways on the tiled surround of the swimming-pool. Suddenly, I remembered the small swish I had heard distantly when I left the cover of the trees.

'Observe, Mr. Shand,' said Kesselring eagerly.

I stared down. Paula cried out briefly. There was a swift running ripple along the surface, then a black fin cleaved the water and there was an obscene flash of white turning.

Kesselring said. 'For you, my friends, a midnight bathe — with company.'

We were looking down at a mako shark.

15

Kesselring's hand had sped in and out of his double-breasted jacket. Now it was aiming a made-to-order .22 Sarmco match pistol. They cost from £150 upwards and fire only one shot, but he wouldn't need more than one. Svendstrom was still holding his pump-gun and Bowles had another .22 — a single-shot Hammerli.

'If you make a break for it you will still go into the pool alive, since we shall not shoot to kill,' said Kesselring. 'On the other hand, you may prefer — most understandably — to postpone your aquatic execution. Walk!'

He nodded at the tiled surround. We went along it with the buoyant *élan* of prisoners on the last walk to the death house in Sing Sing. Midway down the line of cabins Kesselring stopped. Belligi yanked two doors open and stood back, grinning.

'Inside, my friends,' rapped Kesselring.

We went in, one in each of two cabins, side by side.

'You have perhaps an hour for sombre contemplation,' Kesselring said. He sighed falsely. 'I regret that the majority of us will be unable to remain for the sport, but it is necessary for us to leave very soon.'

The cabin doors clicked and Kesselring called softly: 'Tony, who looks after my little villa, will attend to matters in our enforced absence. You *amico*, will go first . . . for Tony desires to entertain Miss Vincent in complete privacy.'

Their footsteps were fading in the distance before either of us said anything and then it was Paula who spoke. 'Dale, my darling — we're finished!'

'Not for sixty minutes.' I said it without conviction or even hope and she knew it.

'God in heaven, these men must be sub-human,' Paula whispered. 'To . . . to . . . '

'Quit thinking about it.' I tried the door, but it had a double-locking device of some kind and the old trick with the thin wedge of celluloid wouldn't work. I climbed on to a wood seat and managed to get my head over the top of the partition between the cabins. She looked up at me, her face emptied of colour.

I said: 'Christ — I've landed you in something.' I stretched a hand down the other side of the partition and wound fingers round hers.

'It's not your fault, Dale. I came into this because I wanted to.'

'Don't waste time talking. We've got to figure a way out.'

'How *can* we?'

'We have to try, it's that or . . . '

A line of cabins, like death cells. A white-painted party wall separating one from the other and you could just get your head over the top. Even if I could drop down into Paula's cubicle we'd still be prisoners, waiting for the deadline.

My left foot slipped and the upper part of my body thumped against the partition. Something sagged, only slightly but it sagged. I pulled my head back and moved a hand along the wall. It had been built up with joined vertical planks and then painted.

From the other side, Paula's voice: 'What is it, Dale?'

I leaned against the loose plank, using increasing pressure. It began to give under the impact. I had to do it slowly, almost imperceptibly, but there would still be a crunching sound when it finally gave way. It probably wouldn't be heard inside the villa — but just the same, I judged the moment and synchronised a fit of coughing with it. The plank fell inwards and Paula stopped it banging down on the cabin floor.

In the next instant I was through and standing with her. I looked at my watch. It said 11.37 p.m. Not much time, but it might be enough. For what? I didn't know clearly. Something, though. Like getting through to the cabin beyond Paula's because only the two we were in had been locked.

I explored the next partition wall. There was no more loose woodwork. Maybe I could smash a way through — but they'd hear that all right.

There was still one chance, though. They had taken my gun, but I had the detached plank — if I could use it fast enough when Belligi came.

A car engine hummed in the distance and was gone. Kesselring leaving in the Maserati with the others, going — where? It didn't matter, not now. Nothing mattered except waiting for Belligi. I looked again at my watch. Five minutes before midnight.

Footsteps, moving slowly and deliberately, as if he was savouring every inch of the way. The footsteps ceased — outside the cabin they had shut me in.

A key turned twice in the double lock. Then his voice.

'Outside, Signor Shand — and remember I have the gun, eh?' He laughed delightedly.

The door opened inwards. He stopped laughing.

'I said to come outside, Shand . . . ' The voice had become a rasp of sound.

I was holding the plank sideways in a direct line from my body, waiting. I wasn't even breathing.

The thick voice blared: 'You are reluctant, *amico*. Okay, I come in for you with a bullet!'

He stepped in through the doorway with the pump-gun. A screech froze on his mouth. He wheeled in the confined space of the cabin — and simultaneously I drove the plank straight at him, like a battering-ram. He saw it coming in the penultimate moment and twisted. The plank crunched into his right shoulder instead of his chest. The Winchester slammed into the wall of the cubicle while he flailed backwards through the doorway, spinning round.

I tore through the gap after him. He crouched low down and came at me with a fist swinging viciously upwards. I feinted and let him have it — a hooker which jerked his head right back. Another screech came from him, but he wasn't done yet. He sidestepped, making a sweeping arc with his right hand. There was a glitter of blue steel as he closed in. I lunged at an angle, then tore in with one hand locked on his wrist, forcing it up.

We were swaying to and fro, fighting

silently without quarter or scruple. His knee drove up. I swung the lower part of my body away, enough to miss the sickening impact. But the movement had slackened the purchase I had on his wrist.

He laughed, a sound that was like no laugh I had ever heard. He ripped his hand completely free and drove the blade down for my stomach. I pulled right out and went down on my back.

Belligi's face was a ravaged mask of triumph. He made his travestied laugh again — and swung his foot full to my face.

I half-rolled — and caught his ankle with both hands. He lost his balance and hit the tiled walk with his back. I piled on top of him. Now we were locked together, rolling over and over. He spread fingers over my mouth, thrusting my head far back. I gave him a knee, in the solar plexus. The fearful pressure of his hand eased marginally — then he was clawing at my eyes. From somewhere close Paula screamed.

I jerked my face away, missing the tearing fingers by inches. But he had put

209

everything he had in the desperate surge across my body and it sent him slithering over and beyond me . . . over the smooth tiled surround of the pool and straight down into the water.

Paula cried out again. I came back on my feet, tottering almost on the brink. I felt her grab me, though I wasn't falling.

We stared down into the pool.

Belligi's tormented face showed. The black fin cleaved above the surface . . . then a vast grinning face full of teeth. There was a single dreadful scream, a sudden flurry of water, darkly green . . . then reddening.

I held Paula against me, turning her face from the sliced body which had been Tony Belligi.

16

I sent her into the villa and dragged what was left of him out of the pool. There might be a chance that he was still alive, but he wasn't. The ripped-open body was appalling to see, and for the first time in my life I was sick. I covered the body and went out into the villa.

Paula looked ashen. For a long moment she clung to me. I found the brandy and made two stiff drinks. Twenty minutes later I stopped the Fiat on the road back to Rome and called the police, mastering enough passable Italian to tell them there was a dead man by the swimming-pool at the Villa Bella.

The fellow who answered started yelling down the line, but I didn't stop to listen. Maybe they could trace the call — but by that time we would be back in Rome.

I called Bond when we got there. If he was happy he was hiding the fact with aplomb.

'All right, I can guess what you think.' I said. 'I've made a balls of everything.'

He chuckled then. 'I said that to you once before, didn't I? On reflection, though, I don't think that, this time. I'd say you've come out of it pretty damned well, old boy.'

'Thanks.'

'Don't be gloomy — Kesselring will be on his way to Engand totally oblivious of the fact that you are very much alive. I think Carruthers will regard that as a situation capable of being turned to some advantage. I take it you'll both be flying back immediately?'

'Yes, there's nothing to stay on here for.'

Bond said thoughtfully: 'Kesselring and his friends will probably be on the 1.30 a.m. flight. There's another at three. I can fix it for you, even to the extent of cancelling somebody else's booking.'

'Fix one in the morning, preferably about noon,' I told him. 'It's not urgent — and we need some sleep.'

'All right. I'll drop round for you at ten-thirty.'

'Fine.' I hung up and walked with Paula into the bar. It was one in the morning and the guy behind the counter looked about ready to call time, until he saw us — or perhaps he just liked looking at Paula.

'Two *negronis, signor — signorina*?'

'Two *negronis*,' I said. 'We can take them into the foyer if you want to shut the bar.'

'*Signor!*' The suggestion seemed to outrage his finest feelings. 'I remain until you depart.'

I palmed him a thousand lire note and we sat in a corner of his bar.

Paula said: 'I ought to be falling asleep where I'm sitting, but I feel more awake than ever.'

'Too much has been happening — you're keyed-up.'

'And you?'

'Much the same, I guess.'

She fell silent, then suddenly shivered. I closed a hand on hers. 'Don't think about it, Paula. He was going to kill me.'

'Both of us, after . . . '

'It's all over. Put it out of your mind.'

Time passed. I got two more drinks and we took them into the foyer. The bartender's head was nodding; he had probably been on duty since about nine in the morning.

The double doors to the street were wide open, but it was still warm — the pervading warmth which engulfs all Italy before the chill damp winds of the *tramontana* sweep down the land from the distant North.

Paula said: 'Tell me all about yourself, Dale.'

'I'd rather hear about you.'

She lay back in her chair, looking at me. 'Well, I'm twenty-nine and both my parents are dead — a car crash on the M5 the year before last. They were going on holiday to the West Country. I had originally intended going with them but a job I had applied for came up, so I didn't.'

'I'm truly sorry about the crash, but I'm glad you weren't in it. You must have felt desolated.'

'Yes, I loved them,' she answered simply. 'Our home was at Tarporley, near

Chester, and afterwards I went to live in London. With six O-levels and three languages, plus a commerce diploma, I got a post with the Foreign Office. Probably it was all my fault, but I couldn't see myself settling in the climate there. So I left and tried various things.'

'Such as?'

'I worked on a farm for a while. Then I got a secretarial job with a road construction outfit and after that I became an airline stewardess. About that time I had a bad emotional upset.' For a moment she hesitated, but went on: 'I was in love, or thought I was. I also thought he was wonderful. Unfortunately, I found out he was already married.'

'You mean fortunately.'

'Yes.' She eyed me directly and said: 'I felt a bloody bitch, even though I didn't know and wouldn't have known but for sheer chance. He never told me. It was the way he lied and cheated that really threw me. I was in a pretty bad state. I quit the airline and just on impulse I took the job at the block of flats.'

'You're worth better than that, Paula.'

'Yes, I know. I suppose it was a sort of temporary escape route. I simply wanted to get clean away from everything to do with my past life. Then you walked in. Give me a cigarette, Dale.'

I passed a new twenty packet across and lit one myself.

'It's your turn now,' she said.

'I'll make it brief. Small town boy from the Middle West looking for fame and fortune in New York, like a legion before me. Newspaper work, which I liked. Job as an assistant investigator in the District Attorney's office, which I also liked — only I'm not a good team man and I stubbed my big feet on a few important toes. In the end, I quit to become a private eye. Not the best way to make a living and there were times when I didn't make it.'

'Go on.'

'Finally, I started to get better-paid assignments. One case took me to England. I'd been here before, with the U.S. Army, and I always liked the country. Through a combination of circumstances, I decided to open up here.'

'You mean you've an office and a staff and everything?'

'An office and a girl who runs it for me.'

'Oh — a girl?'

'Yes, her name's Nancy. She used to operate the switchboard in the apartment house where I lived in New York — in fact, I've kept the place on.'

'I suppose she's pretty?' said Paula meditatively.

'Very.'

'I see.'

'No, you don't. I'm not having an affair with her and never have had.'

'But you brought her to England with you.'

'She knows more about the way I operate than anyone I can think of, and she always wanted to work with me. When I decided to come over here I couldn't think of anyone more capable of minding the office.'

'I'll bet she minds you, too.'

'Why, do I look like a man who needs minding?'

'All men need minding. Nice men,

anyway. How old are you?'

'Nearly forty.'

'And you've never married?'

'No.'

'I don't know that I want marriage now,' she said, almost as if to herself. 'It's so chancy. Or perhaps it's just because I had this experience. I dare say it's put me off. Also, I like my independence.'

There didn't seem to be anything to say and I didn't try to find anything. Paula mashed out her cigarette and said: 'It's late, I'm going up.'

We got into the elevator and I thumbed the button for the second floor. She seemed preoccupied. So was I. It was too much to expect that the reasons were indentical.

The car clanged to a stop, the doors parted and we walked in silence down the corridor. Our doors faced one another. She stopped outside hers, opened it and turned fully towards me. 'Have I told you all you want to know about me?' she asked.

'I don't know.' Without consciously thinking about it, I said: 'You can't know everything in so little time.'

'No.' She looked at me again, her eyes very clear. I had no notion of what was in them. 'Don't you want to find out?' she added.

I circled an arm round her and went into the room and closed the door and got lights on, not all of them. A long time later I knew much more about her.

17

The temperature was pushing up into the middle eighties when the BOAC jet came in at London Airport. In George Carruthers' handsome room at New Scotland Yard it was sagging down towards zero. I could feel it the moment we walked in late the next afternoon.

Carruthers went over everything that had happened, asked all the right questions, made the seemingly right answers. He was bland and smiling and imperturbable, but there was something wrong. For minutes I couldn't pin it down; then, suddenly, I realised what it was. He was uncomfortable.

Finally, I said outright: 'Something's happened, hasn't it?'

The old jauntiness came back, briefly. 'You don't miss anything, Shand, I'll say that for you,' he remarked.

'What is it?'

He took a cigar from a box and pushed

the box across to me. I shook my head, waiting.

Carruthers changed his mind and put the cigar back. He started speaking slowly, as if deciding or choosing what to say. That wasn't in character, either, because he had always known what to say.

'I'm afraid you've rather scared the quarry, Shand,' he said at last. 'I don't mean you've bungled things — the course of events left you with no alternative. On that basis you did well — damned well. But the fact remains that as a result Kesselring has been put on his guard. You must see that.'

'I can see it up to a point,' I said. 'But he doesn't know you're on to the plot against the President. He merely thinks you suspect him of stirring up student trouble.'

'Kesselring has one of the first-class brains in the espionage field. Your intervention and the fact that he knows of your connection with us will have told him all he needs to know about our real suspicions.'

'Maybe. I'm not fully convinced of

that. Another thing — he now supposes that both Miss Vincent and myself are dead.'

Carruthers shrugged. 'It won't take him long to find out that you're not.'

'Yes, but now he's almost certainly in London. There's nothing to prevent your department putting the arm on him.'

Carruthers studied his beautifully-tended hands. When he looked up he said incisively: 'We're not ready for that. I told you we need evidence and we haven't got it.'

'Meaning I failed to get it?'

'If you put it that way, yes.'

'He tried to have us killed, Mr. Carruthers,' said Paula mildly.

'I'm not doubting that for one second, Miss Vincent — but my department has learned not to be unduly worried by attempts on the lives of its agents.' He smiled thinly. 'That probably sounds callous, but it is necessary to say it. Such things are occupational hazards. Our single purpose is to obtain sufficent evidence to scoop-up Kesselring and his associates. Besides, your experience took

222

place in a foreign country, outside our jurisdiction.'

'All right,' I growled. 'I take the point — but what follows?'

Carruthers eyed me levelly. 'I think,' he said, 'I think that for the time being it will be better if both Miss Vincent and yourself cease to be identified with our investigations.'

'I stared. 'Why?'

'It's reasonably clear, isn't it? Kesselring knows you both. Any move you now make must necessarily suffer from this disadvantage.'

'He knows Bond, but you haven't sacked *him*.'

'The circumstances are not the same . . . '

'He also knows about your department and probably knows about you — to that extent you work under a similar handicap.'

'You're missing the point — that he has been personally involved with you, Shand.' He stood up rather abruptly. 'I'm damned sorry — but, for the time being at least, I'm taking you off this.'

'You mean you're just taking me off and never mind the time being qualification.'

'I haven't said that. If you care to know, I have a considerable regard for your abilities and it is more than likely that we shall want to work with you in the future.'

'But not in the immediate future.'

'I'm sorry — but, well, no.'

Almost boyishly, he put out a hand and I took it briefly. 'You have an assignment of your own within the next day or two,' he said. 'When you're through with that come and see me again. Miss Vincent, too.'

We went out and sat in my car.

'Well,' said Paula, 'that's that — the end of a beautiful relationship.'

I didn't answer and she went on: 'There's something bothering you, I can tell.'

'Yeah — I don't get it.'

'What?'

'His entire attitude. It's not like Carruthers to throw you out in the middle of an investigation.'

'Perhaps we *have* made things a bit

difficult for his department?'

'Complications are nearly always inevitable. Somewhere along the line, one or more of us were bound to come up against Kesselring.'

Paula touched my arm. 'Are you saying that Mr. Carruthers was simply looking for any old excuse to get rid of you or us?'

'No. he isn't that kind of guy.'

'Then what on earth *do* you think?'

'I think he's been got at by someone — one of the highups.'

'If it's like that why couldn't he just say so?'

'Professional ethics or whatever. He was probably asked to play it that way.'

'You're just guessing, you know.'

I grinned. 'Making deductions from revealed circumstances is how I prefer to put it. Another thing — at no point did George Carruthers offer criticism of what we did. Therefore, his attitude can be explained only on the premise that somebody in the top brass figures we goofed and wants us removed. We've become a couple of expendables.'

'But surely Mr. Carruthers could have resisted?'

'I'd say he probably did, but was over-ruled.'

'So now we're out in the cold?'

'Not necessarily.'

Paula turned a startled face towards me. 'For heaven's sake, you're not going it alone, are you?'

'Frankly, I don't know. But I'm going to think about it.'

'Mr. Carruthers will be vexed.'

'Well, he — or the fellow above him — have annoyed *me*.'

'If you start acting on your own you won't have any protection . . . ' began Paula.

'We haven't had that, anyway. If you become an agent, even semi-officially, you're out on a limb all the time.'

'We might find ourselves fighting not only Kesselring but the entire British secret service.'

'*I* might find myself doing that — not you.'

'I'm in this with you.'

'Not this time. I can't have you running

that kind of risk.' I started the car and added: 'Anyway, I still haven't decided what I'm going to do. I'll take a little time out to think. In the meantime, I'll drive you home.'

When we got to her apartment she said: 'Are you coming in?'

'Not now, Paula. I'm going to my office.'

'And the beautiful Nancy?' she said mockingly.

It was after five when I got there. Nancy was getting ready to leave. 'Did you have a nice trip?' she asked.

'You've got the wrong word.'

I told her what had happened and the first thing she said was: 'I didn't know you had company.'

'Meaning feminine company?'

'Any kind of company,' answered Nancy, not convincingly. She went on: 'And now Mr. Carruthers has taken you off the case. I think you're well out of it.'

'That's what you thought about Amanda Chester.'

'I was right then and I'm right now. Which reminds me — Mr. Kenning wants to see you on Sunday for a final conference on the industrial assignment. Four-thirty at his home.'

'I'll be there.'

She eyed me thoughtfully and said: 'The best thing you can do, apart from forgetting all this security business, is to go home and have a nice long refreshing sleep.'

'Yes, Nancy,' I said meekly.

She appeared to hesitate for a moment. Then she said: 'I worry about you.'

'You shouldn't.'

'Why shouldnt I?' she demanded. 'I've known you a long time and I work in close relationship with you. I just don't like your getting mixed-up in dubious cases which offer all the disadvantages of the profession and none of the benefits.'

'You're becoming a conformist, playing all the smooth angles.'

'You oughtn't to despise them, Mr. Shand — they bring you a substantial income and don't let anyone ever tell you that money isn't important.'

'I've never said that, Nancy, but . . . ' I shrugged.

'Well, don't stay late at the office brooding over Mr. Carruthers — it's a waste of time now,' she said.

In fact, I stayed there for upwards of half an hour after she had gone. She was right, of course, and so was Paula. If I carried on independently I'd be bucking the British Intelligence as well as Kesselring. No protection, no help, no money — no anything. Better call time on yourself, Shand. It all made sense, but . . .

I felt oddly restless, disinclined either to go to my flat or to seek company. I wanted to be alone. I went out, walking steadily, barely aware of the early evening crowds. In fact, I was barely aware of the direction I was taking until I had got beyond Piccadilly Circus and was approaching Grosvenor Square.

There seemed to be a hell of a commotion just ahead. When I reached the square I understood what it was — another demonstration converging on the U.S. Embassy. Long hair and short skirts, beards and banners, chanted slogans instead of rational thought. Well-meaning people

. . . and an organised hard core of the less well-intentioned. And everywhere the police — outnumbered, phlegmatic, doing a difficult job not for big rewards. They must be sick of constantly recurring mob hysteria with the ever-present undertow of violence which sometimes erupted into the reality of the boot in the face of a pinioned cop or the lighted cigarette thrust under the belly of a horse.

I turned to go back the way I had come, but there was now no space behind me. More and more people were pushing in. I was swept forward by a human tide. Then *they* had to stop because the square was now almost literally jammed. The police were strung out. Keeping the militant vanguard from getting close to the Embassy.

A girl who looked no more than seventeen screamed: 'Fascist pigs!'

The boy who was with her threw a toliet roll over the heads of those immediately in front of him, aiming at a mounted policeman. The roll uncoiled, wrapping itself round the horse's head.

Away to the right a crowd of students

thrust forward with improvised placards telling the Yanks to go home. One of the group, a tall lad with dark hair sloping down the sides of his pale face, suddenly stopped. He was staring fixedly towards where I stood and I had an odd sensation that he knew me — though I had no recollection of ever having seen him before.

They were chanting 'Ho! Ho! Ho-Chi-Minh!', as if he was still alive. The pressure from behind almost toppled the boy. He turned and yelled: 'There's one of them — one of the American imperialist aggressors!'

The others looked round, uncertainly. He stopped to pick up a stone and hurled it straight at me. If I hadn't been watching it would have taken me full in the face. As it was I went sideways very fast and the stone sailed past me, missing whoever was behind. I heard it hit the ground as I jumped at him.

I just had time to deliver a swift uppercut before a posse of police, materialising like magic apparently from nowhere, swept in. The air was full of shouts, yells and assorted confusion — in the midst of which the young fellow, who had reeled back into the arms of his friends, vanished in a whirl of mixed bodies. By the time the bluecoats were at close quarters his chums had smuggled him out of sight.

The heavy hand of the law fell on Shand instead . . .

18

It is the thoughtful view of most acute observers that a man rarely looks his best after a night in the cells, and by the following morning I was able to testify to the validity of this judgement.

Maybe I could have got Carruthers to bail me out. I might even have used his influence to get the whole thing dropped. I didn't even try. He had taken me off the case and if getting myself arrested was going to vex him — let it.

All I did was get a message to Paula who came round to see me and thought I was being obstinate. Well, I was.

There were eleven other arrests in Grosvenor Square. Four who had been in trouble before for disorderly conduct and carrying offensive weapons were given short-term jail sentences. The rest of us were fined varying amounts — £5 in my case.

When I walked out of court Paula

was waiting for me. 'My, what a sight you look,' she said. 'I think you need a drink.'

'Well, they're open,' I growled.

'No, we'll go to your flat,' she said decisively. 'You can have a nice hot bath and a shave and change your clothes and then weep on my shoulder.'

We went in a taxi. Fifteen minutes later I was feeling rather less like something rejected by the pure food committee. I came out of the bathroom to find her waiting with the drinks on a tray.

She patted the settee and said: 'Now sit down and tell mother all about it.'

'I told you last night.'

'Tell me again.'

I did and she said: 'The boy who threw the stone — what makes you think he knew you?'

'I'm damned if I know. but it was in his face — the way he looked at me.'

'He might've seen you when you called at the college.'

'It's possible, I suppose, though I don't recall noticing him. I'll try to find out, though. The student I talked to there might know something. Or does it matter?'

'Perhaps not. Have you decided what you're going to do — I mean about this whole business?'

'Yeah, I'm going back to Carruthers. He's holding something back, I'm certain of it and . . . ' That was as far as I got when the phone rang. It was Carruthers.

'You're on cue,' I said. 'I was just talking about you.'

'I rang your office. Your secretary said you hadn't turned up. I guessed where you'd be.'

'Meaning you know about last night and the court proceedings?'

'Naturally. Why the devil didn't you contact me?'

'I thought you'd prefer not to be involved. It might have embarrassed you.'

'You're lying, Shand,' he answered amiably. 'You must have known that I might be more embarrassed by your appearance in court.'

'All right, so I deliberately embarrassed you.'

'Your name will be in the papers and

that, taken in conjunction with your recent activities on our behalf, is somewhat irritating.'

'You rather irritated me yesterday,' I said sourly.

'Yes, I realise that. Unfortunately, I had no other course open to me. It is even probable that we owe you a more detailed explanation. Can you come round right away? I want you to meet the Minister himself.'

'I suppose he's behind my being removed from the investigation.'

'Are you coming along or not?'

'In an hour, will that do?'

'Yes — though I see no reason why you can't come earlier.'

'I like the idea of keeping one of Her Majesty's Ministers waiting,' I said. 'This one, anyway.'

Carruthers made a small sound that could have been a dry chuckle and hung up.

I dropped Paula at her flat and showed-up on time. Carruthers said: 'We're seeing the Minister in his room.'

'I take it he *is* behind all this?'

'He'll tell you himself,' Carruthers rejoined.

We went through an oak-panelled door into a large room whose heavy Victorian furniture, which made it a sort of cross between an office and a study, suggested a long line of occupants stretching back to the halcyon days when the British happily solved their foreign problems with a naval gunboat.

The latest tenant was Foley Aynsworth, a tall greying man with flat cheeks, a long thin face and the mannered charm of a diplomat of the old school. I had been prepared to dislike him on sight, but it wasn't going to be so easy as that. Not because of the charm he could probably turn on and off at will but because the blue eyes which regarded me were clearly those of a man of integrity. And something else. Unless I was making a wild guess, they were the eyes of a man with trouble on his mind.

'Sit down, Mr. Shand,' he said. 'Would you care for a drink?'

'Thanks — whisky.'

We all had whisky. Aynsworth asked me

about myself, my work, America and whether I liked England. Then, without change of tone or emphasis, he said: 'Carruthers tells me you are a man of considerable resource. You co-operated both with us and our American opposites two years ago, with marked distinction.'

I didn't answer and he resumed: 'That was all shortly before I was given this post. You are perhaps thinking rather badly of my recent directive to Carruthers?'

'Not perhaps, Minister.'

He smiled, a long thin smile. 'You are frank, Mr. Shand.'

'My candour doesn't matter. I'm interested in hearing why you did it.'

Aynsworth sipped his whisky, put the glass down and said: 'Carruthers has — ah — persuaded me that you are entitled to a rather more detailed explanation than, on my instruction, he offered you yesterday.'

Carruthers, who was sitting almost opposite me, glanced across, then away. I had a sudden impression that he was troubled, too.

Aynsworth seemed to be searching for the right words. It must have been ten seconds before he spoke again. Then he said slowly: 'You will appreciate that the investigations this department is making involve the highest security requirements.'

'If you're asking me to keep whatever knowledge I have to myself you're wasting your time and mine,' I said shortly. 'The request is unnecessary and uncomplimentary.'

For a moment he seemed in danger of losing his trained urbanity. Then he got it fully back. 'You misunderstand me, Shand. I had no such request in mind. The position is that we are involved in matters of what Shakespeare calls great moment. In these circumstances it is necessary to exercise the utmost care. There must be no risk of the enemy being forewarned. Unfortunately, your own recent involvement places you in a position which I judge to be detrimental to the overall conduct of our investigations.'

'In a nutshell, you think I'm in the way?'

'Effectively, yes.'

'I don't see it.'

'There is also the new point that what happened last night and in the magistrate's court this morning ought surely to convince you that your activities are scarely likely to further the success of our mission.'

'I don't see that, either. I'm still the same man — the same qualities, the same defects, the same overall competence which your department found useful two years ago.'

'Your professionalism is not in question, I was under the impression that I had made that clear. It is — how shall I put it? — your apparent tendency to be incident-prone.'

'I didn't arrange any of the incidents, they arranged themselves, Minister. And what occurred last night wasn't due to any ill-judged action of mine. I was attacked without warning by a young demonstrator in Grosvenor Square.'

He moved a hand as if to dismiss the point. He did it without looking directly at me or at anything in particular.

'There's something strange about that, too,' I said. 'The fellow who threw the stone knew me.'

Carruthers looked up sharply. 'You didn't say that in court.'

'I kept it back. It wouldn't have made any difference.'

Carruthers was about to say something when Aynsworth said, with the first show of irritability: 'What has a brawling student to do with all this?'

'*I didn't say he was a student,*' I answered.

He stood up quickly, going across the handsome, old-fashioned room to the big mahogany sideboard. 'Perhaps you would care for another drink . . . '

I knew what he was going to do. He *had* to do it, had to place himself between my line of vision and the side-board. But he was too late. As he moved I pushed my chair back at an angle and saw what he wanted to hide. A framed photograph of a boy maybe nineteen or twenty years old.

It was the face of the student in Grosvenor Square.

19

We were back in Carruthers' office. Logan had joined us. A girl secretary came in with a buff-coloured folder.

Carruthers told her: 'Don't come back in any circumstances until I send for you. Margaret.' He made his disarming smile. 'A rather important conference. All right?'

'Yes, Mr. Carruthers,' She went away and closed the door quietly but firmly.

Evenly, Carruthers said: 'Now, Shand — what do you know?'

'I imagine you've already made an accurate deduction.'

'Never mind what I've deduced, my dear chap.'

'You want me to tell you something, though I'm no longer to be trusted with the investigation?'

'Damn it, Shand, don't talk balls.' I had never heard him use the word before and from him it sounded odd.

Logan, who was sitting in his charateristic semi-dislocated attitude in a leather armchair, permitted himself a dry chuckle.

'This isn't funny,' Carruthers said. 'Shand knows something, something specific about the student who attacked him. It was a student?'

'Yeah — your Minister told you.'

'He slipped and you obligingly pointed it out to him, didn't you? Are you going to level with us, as you Americans say?'

'All right. The young fellow who went for me at the demonstration was a ringer for the one in that picture in Aynsworth's room.'

Carruthers smiled bleakly. 'Let's not mince words. Are you saying they are one and the same?'

'I'm quite sure of it.'

'I'm willing to accept that. It doesn't necessarily imply anything.' For the first time since I had known him, Carruthers spoke without confidence.

'You have to consider the balance of probabilities,' I said. 'Kesselring knew you were gunning for him before I even met him — he let me know that much because he never believed I'd escape. Even if you discount that, you're still faced with the fact that they knew we were going to Rome. I'm saying outright that young Aynsworth leaked that information.'

For a long moment Carruthers sat there drumming his fingers on the desk. Finally, he said: 'Yes.'

'I thought you were reluctant to believe that.'

'Foley Aynsworth is my Minister, a man of absolute professional and personal probity. If I seemed reluctant it was a natural reaction, Shand. But not one to be persisted in. I accept the reality.'

'I still haven't direct proof. It could be a double.'

'No, the coincidence is too complete.' He half-turned and added: 'What do you think, Logan?'

'I think we'd better find young Aynsworth and confront him with Shand.'

'Yes. It'll have to be handled discreetly. We don't want any of this to become public property.' Carruthers touched his clipped moustache. 'And that's not merely to save his father embarrassment.'

'You want him brought in and questioned privately so that none of it gets back to Kesselring?' I said.

'Quite. Perhaps you'll see to it, Logan? The boy doesn't live at home, he's in a hall of residence. Just get him to come along — say, about five this afternoon. I'll arrange for his father to be present. It will not, I'm afraid, be pleasant for him.'

'He'll have to resign?' asked Logan.

'I'm not sure. It will be partly up to Aynsworth himself. But in all the circumstances, something's got to happen. How about you, Shand?'

'Yeah, how about me?'

'Oh, just that you're back with us, if you're still interested,' replied Carruthers imperturbably. 'I'm taking that decision without reference to the Minister. Also in all the circumstances.''

Logan produced a second dry chuckle. 'I'll say this for Shand — he's a hard man to include out.'

'By the way,' I said. 'Ellery — what's he doing?'

'Lying low,' answered Logan. 'We're

letting him — for the time being. Not that we've a thing on him, in any case — so far as association with Kesselring goes.'

I remembered the phone conversation I had overheard in Ellery's flat. Wednesday was the set day and this was Wednesday — but they wouldn't be meeting at the set place. If they met at all it would be somewhere else.

Logan said: 'We've got Ellery under observation. Can't promise to be within sight of him all the twenty-four hours, though. He might dodge us for an hour or so. We're not infallible.'

'I still don't see Ellery in the kind of set-up Kesselring is promoting,' I said.

Carruthers looked at me. 'Everything points to his being in direct association. What's on your mind?'

'I'm not sure. I just have a feeling that Ellery is playing some game of his own.'

'If he is, Kesselring is quite liable to have him removed — permanently,' replied Carruthers dryly.

★   ★   ★

I went out, but not to my office or back to Paula. I had a sudden notion to look up Peter Guthrie again. I had liked the look of him — the kind of student this or any other country needed. But he might know more about the nihilistic fringe than he had mentioned or remembered at the time.

I found him coming from a lecture. 'Why, hello, Mr. Shand,' he said. 'What is it this time?'

'Can we talk in private?'

'If you want.' He opened a door into an ante-room and looked at me curiously. 'I haven't a lot of time — can you make it brief?'

'Very brief. Do you know any other young fellows here who are associated with the group to which Franklin belongs?'

He looked slightly ill-at-ease. 'I don't know that I ought to implicate any of my colleagues,' he said at length.

I hesitated only seconds. Then I told him — not everything but enough. He stared incredulously. 'You must be joking . . . '

'I'm being very serious, Mr. Guthrie. If you do know anyone involved with this group it might help more than you realise.'

He ran fingers through his heavy hair and said: 'Phil Bennion, Charles Marley and Derek Aynsworth.' A look came on his face 'I think . . . I'm not positive but I think Derek has just gone to meet somone.'

'Where?' I shrugged. 'Obviously, you won't know the answer to that.'

'Well, as a matter of fact, I do. I heard him on the phone. He said he'd be on the westbound platform at Leicester Square Tube station. I was passing and happened to overhear it. I thought it was a damned funny place to be meeting anyone.'

'When did he leave?'

'About a couple of minutes before you came.'

'How?'

'I think he was going for a bus.'

'Thanks,' I said.

'I say, I hope I haven't said anything that . . . ' But I didn't stay to listen.

I hadn't brought my car. I caught a taxi

to the Cranbourne Street entrance to the Underground and ran down the escalator to the westbound platform. Plenty of people standing around or strolling up and down, but Derek Aynsworth wasn't among them. An illuminated sign announced: *Next train, Uxbridge Line*. Not that it meant anything to me because I didn't know which line he was travelling on — if any.

The train loomed out of the black mouth of the tunnel. The crowd surged forward, the sliding doors opened and closed and moments later the last coach vanished, leaving the platform empty — but not for long. It filled up again, but there was still no sign of him.

Then suddenly, he was there — some distance from me, under the *Way Out* sign. His gaze darted over the crowd, as if he was looking for someone. I half-turned my face so that he wouldn't see me. The destination sign switched to *Next train, Hounslow Line*. Aynsworth shouldered his way through the almost opaque mass of passengers — and at that moment a figure came on the platform.

It was Svendstrom . . .

He stepped neatly sideways, flattening his back against a wall map of the Underground network, holding a newspaper up to his face. Aynsworth was still looking up and down the jammed platform. The distant thunder of the approaching train welled from the tunnel and the crowd began to press forward in a sort of ragged wave.

Svendstrom dropped the newspaper. Now he had huge rounded sunglasses on his face, making him virtually un-recognisable if I hadn't already seen him. There was a small cleared space between him and Aynsworth, about the only one left on the platform. He slid out fast from the wall.

I couldn't get to Aynsworth in time. I was almost literally pinned down by the crowd — and Svendstrom was right behind him now.

I yelled at the top of my voice: 'Aynsworth — *look out!*'

The yell was half lost in the mounting rumble of the incoming train. He heard me, but not fully in time. Even as his head jerked round, Svendstrom lunged straight at him — his turned right shoulder slamming Aynsworth like a wedge.

For a second the boy swayed on the rim of the platform. His body seemed to hang grotesquely outwards like a buckled lamp standard.

Then he plunged headlong on to the track as the train roared out of the tunnel.

20

Carruthers said: 'I've told the Minister. He's at the hospital now. It'll not be a pleasant sight.'

'No. One of the boy's legs was completely severed and his spine was badly injured.'

'How did they get him out?'

'A guy from the London Ambulance Service did it — they ought to give him a medal.' The power had been shut off while he crawled into the pit and held Aynsworth still. Then they got the power on again and the train moved slowly over them. The live rail runs against the tunnel wall, but if the boy had made a violent spasmodic jerk the ambulance man could have been crushed.

Derek Aynsworth was alive when they got him on a stretcher, but only minutes later he was dead.

'You did your best, Shand.' said

Carruthers quietly. 'I'm going to tell the Minister that.'

'I'm only sorry he didn't jump clear when I shouted — but it was all over in seconds.'

'You're sure it was Svendstrom?'

'Completely sure.'

Logan said: 'We've alerted every division — squad cars, pandas, the lot. Why do you think they did it?'

'I'd say young Aynsworth had also become expendable. Not drugs this time. Something else.'

'He might have begun to suspect the *bona fides* of these men?'

'Or overheard something that caused him to think. We'll probably never know now. But it was Svendstrom who knocked him under the train and it was cold-blooded murder all right.'

'Could he have seen you?' queried Carruthers.

'It's possible, but I don't believe he did. I'm almost certain. Why?'

'Oh, just that you'd be next in line for the execution squad,' replied Carruthers impassively.

'I've already been in it — also Paula Vincent,' I said dryly.

'Yes but they probably don't know yet that you got away. Your name wasn't in the papers — we arranged that. When they do know they'll go after you. Incidentally, if we catch Svendstrom your evidence will convict him.'

'He may be out of the country by now,' reflected Logan.

'I don't think so, there's no reason — if they're unaware that Shand saw the whole thing.'

'Svendstrom must have heard me yell to Aynsworth.' I said slowly. 'But he was in no position to see me. He never even turned — he simply made his getaway.'

The telephone rang. Carruthers answered it. When he put the receiver down he said: 'The Minister wants to see us.'

He was standing silhouetted against the high window of his room. When he turned his face had aged by a decade. Carruthers told him everything.

For a moment Foley Aynsworth looked at me. Then, without speech, he held out a hand. It was colder than ice.

He sat down heavily, motioning to the other chairs. He said simply: 'I'm handing in my resignation to the P.M.'

Nobody spoke. Aynsworth went on. 'I knew my son was involved in militant activities. I thought at first they were just the currently fashionable thing. Then I began to suspect that it might be more than the usual student protest. I thought Shand's investigations might harm Derek. So I had Shand removed from the scene. I hoped to talk to my son of whatever he was doing.'

Aynsworth passed a hand across his forehead. 'The fact is that I allowed my feelings as a parent to take precedence over my obligations as Minister. It is impossible for me to carry on.'

Carruthers said: 'I'm sorry, sir. It would have been better had you told me what you feared.'

'I had no specific knowledge, nothing beyond a feeling that Derek was involved in some way which disturbed me. That is, until . . . ' He hesitated, then said: 'Until I realised something else.'

'Your son was in the building when the Rome briefing was given to Shand and Miss Vincent.'

'Yes. He must have betrayed that information. There can be no other possible explanation.'

'Did you tax him with that?'

Aynsworth nodded. 'He would neither confirm nor deny it — but I knew. I ought to have told you. Instead, I betrayed my own trust. And now he is dead. If I had acted differently I might have prevented that . . . God, what am I to tell his mother?'

'The truth, sir,' said Carruthers quietly.

I looked across at Aynsworth and said: 'Did your son have any close friends — friends that you yourself know of, sir?'

'He didn't confide in me, Shand.' Aynsworth made a tired movement with his shoulders. 'The gap between the generations, I suppose . . . it's happening all the time just now.'

'It's always existed, sir.'

'Yes, but not to the same degree. It wasn't simply a failure in communications between us. I sensed active resentment, in my case probably reinforced by the work I do. To my son I was the physical embodiment of the Establishment — which he quite clearly hated.'

'And you know none of his personal friends?'

'None — except Ginny.'

'A girl friend?'

'Yes — Virginia Leeming. Why do you ask?'

'She might know something about his associates. It's not very probable, but she might. Where does she live?'

'She has a flat in Chelsea, off the King's Road. It's in Ventrix Place, I believe.'

'Not a student?'

'No, she's a model for one of the agencies. I don't know which one. I know little about such things.'

I turned to Carruthers. 'I'd like to talk with her. What do you think?'

'No reason why not, Shand.'

I drove there. Ventrix Place was beyond the old Six Bells pub where they used to have jam sessions before the jazz boom of the Fifties; wasn't it Spike

Hughes who immortalised it in *Six Bells Stampede*?

The place was a mews, trendy with touches of psychedelic colour and striped awnings and plants in hanging baskets. Very cute, like Miss Virginia Leeming who appeared to have been poured into her crimson slacks and sky-blue sweater. She had the kind of pared-down looks and long straight hair presently fashionable among the young and almost jet-black eyelids.

I had to ring the bell twice before she heard it on account of the din going on inside — an amalgam of lifted voices and socked-out pop music.

She put her blonde head round the door, pushed a vast wedge of hair off her face and said: 'Just a minute . . . ' She turned and yelled something. The voices modulated into a minor key and the musical uproar died, greatly respected.

'Awfully sorry. Now then?'

I said: 'I believe you're a friend of Derek Aynsworth?'

'Yes.' She let her gaze drift over me. 'I don't seem to remember you . . . '

'You won't remember me at all, Miss Leeming.'

'What do you want, then?'

'Just a talk, about him.'

She held the door open. 'I've got some friends in, but you can join us.'

I went into a wide lounge which spanned the width of the place. There were three boys and as many girls in it. Long hair and short beards. Modish casuals which looked as neat as an unmade bed. Tights and minis, the Pill, in-talk and love-ins. Or are you just being an old grouch, Shand? Probably.

Ginny Leeming waved a careless hand at her friends without introducing them and said: 'We're expecting Derek later.'

'He won't be coming, I'm afraid.'

'Oh?' She eyed me directly. 'Is something wrong?'

'Yes. Hes been in an accident.'

The taller of the young fellows stared. 'You mean he's been badly hurt?'

'He's dead,' I said.

For a moment Ginny Leeming simply stood there, as if the words had made no impact. Then she whispered: 'Oh dear God, no!'

The tall boy said: 'What happened?'

'He fell under a train at Leicester Square Tube station.'

'Give me a drink, Teddy,' she said.

He poured gin and she drank about half of it in one go and turned back to me. 'Who and what are you?'

I told them as much of it as was necessary; just that Aynsworth was mixed-up with some rather odd characters and had gone to meet one of them and been pushed under the train.

They heard me out in silence. Then the one called Teddy said: 'Jesus Christ . . . *murder!*'

I looked at Ginny Leeming. 'If you know anything about what he was involved in I hope you'll tell me.'

Her face had become a trembling white mask. 'I don't know anything about his student activities,' she answered. 'We were just friends . . . well, we slept together, if you want to know.'

'Not necessarily. I simply hoped you might know something of what he was doing. Specifically, where this group he was in with might be found.'

She shook her head. 'He never said much about it. I knew he was connected with some protest movement or other, but so many of them are.'

'This was rather more than the usual protest thing, Miss Leeming.'

'Yes.' She lit a cigarette with shaking hands. 'I suppose so, but I don't know anything about it and neither do my friends. We're none of us involved with the student scene.'

'So far as you are concerned, he was just your boy friend and that's all?'

She nodded. 'We met at some party, about six weeks ago. He was fun, you know. But I know nothing about underground groups and stuff like that . . . ' She broke off.

I said: 'Yes?'

'It's nothing.'

'Suppose you let me be the judge of that.'

'Well, he seemed somewhat preoccupied, last night it was.'

'Didn't you ask him why?'

261

'Well, yes I did. All he would say was that he was worried over the way things were going with some movement he was in with.' She hesitated again, then went on: 'He did say one thing — something about certain people just being in it for money, a lot of money.'

'And he didn't explain that?'

'No, he just said he didn't like it, that's all.'

I turned to the others. They shook their heads, almost in unison. Then the tall boy said: 'Wait a minute — I remember one thing. I saw Derek leaving a house just off Curzon Street, in Westley Crescent. Twenty-three it was. That was last night. I almost bumped into him . . . '

Ginny Leeming stared: 'You didn't tell me that, Teddy.'

'No.' He looked slightly uncomfortable.

'What happened?' I said.

'When I asked him who he'd been calling on he seemed embarrassed. I thought, well . . . ' Teddy shrugged.

'You thought he might have another girl friend, perhaps?'

'Something like that.'

Ginny Leeming laughed, a brittle sound. 'Awfully considerate of you to keep it to yourself, Teddy.'

'I wasn't sure just how attached you were, darling.'

'Not all that attached, I didn't put a halter on him.' She swung round, looking hard at me. 'You think he was calling at this house for a very different reason, Mr. Shand?'

'It's more than possible.'

'One of his peculiar associates?'

'I'll find out, Miss Leeming.'

For a long moment she was silent. Then she flared: 'I hope you find the man who killed Derek — not that it makes much difference now, does it? Murderers don't hang any more.'

'No, but I'd have expected you to oppose capital punishment.'

'Yes, that's right, we all do. Or did. It's rather different when someone you've loved is murdered, though, isn't it?'

'I guess it is, though it doesn't really affect the principle.'

'I don't feel in the humour for academic discussions of principle, Mr.

Shand. Derek was a nice boy, no matter what he'd been silly enough to get into.'

'I'm sure of it,' I said. 'More than that, I think he was killed because he found out the truth, or some of it.'

A shiver possessed her. Then it was gone and she said quietly: 'If anything else comes back to me or I hear anything, I'll get in touch with you.'

'Thanks, Miss Leeming — and once again I'm very sorry.'

I got back in my car and sat there for minutes, thinking. So there was money in it? What money and from whom and how? An idea began to shape far down in my mind. I dragged it out in the open and took a long hard look at it. A crazy idea — or was it? Maybe there was a way to find out.

I meshed the gears and drove to Westley Crescent.

21

It was a very short street, a dead end street of oldish Georgian terraced houses. I found the right one and drove straight past it. At the end of the street, beyond the last house, there was a fairly wide entry. I put the car there and went down it on foot and round the corner, counting the houses back to No. 23. A ginger cat perched on one of the low walls gave me a bland yellow eye and started purring, as if sensing the presence of a friend. There was no other sign of life.

I tried the gate. It was open. I went down a paved yard. The rear door was locked, but the window was half open. I hesitated, but not more than a second, before getting a leg over the sill. Breaking and entering — or, at least, being found on enclosed premises. Any minute now an outraged householder might be reaching for the phone or a weapon in self-defence. But I didn't really think that. I had a sure feeling that the place was empty. I climbed through the window, went along a hall and turned into what looked like a lounge. Still nobody. The place was empty all right.

There was a curved desk under the window. On it was a leather-bound folded blotter and a crimson telephone. I pulled drawers out and looked at what was in them. Writing-paper, envelopes, paper clips, old cheque books fastened with rubber bands, a current one and a book of bank paying-in slips. I opened it and looked at one of the carbon-copy retained pages. It showed that the account was in the name of G. Ellery.

And Derek Aynsworth had been here, in this house. Why? In the light of what had happened, it could only be because he suspected something — and had been foolish enough to confront Garfield Ellery.

I looked again at the paying-in book. The last three entries, all within days of each other, were of £47-10-0, £300 and £430-16-0.

Nice paying-in, but not necessarily

illegal — or even significant. Big money, the late Derek Aynsworth had said. How big?

I had just pushed the drawer back when I heard a key turn in the front door. I went across the hall into what looked like a small spare room, sparsely equipped. If there had been a glass panel let into the front door he'd have seen me, but I already knew there wasn't. I closed the room door until there was no more than a slit view, but it ought to be enough.

Garfield Ellery came into the hall, dropped his hat on a side table and went into the lounge. I could no longer see him, but I could hear him because he was using the phone.

'Eddie? So you're back. The Manchester job went all right, then . . . ' A pause, then: 'Yeh, everything's great here. We're through with Kesselring. I gave him a final tipoff. The Wednesday meeting was called off — but he's paid us out. I don't know where he is and I don't damned well care. The way's clear for the other thing.'

Another pause.

'Yeh — Hatton Garden, just as we planned. No, I can't set the date, Eddie. But have the boys ready. It'll be when Kesselring and his mob move — and I'll know when that is. If we're ready we move at the same time, see?'

Nothing more. I could still hear Ellery in the room, then a hiss like a siphon squirting. I went softly down the hall and out the way I had come in. He didn't hear me.

But I had heard him.

* * *

Carruthers sat in silence until I was through. Then he said meditatively: 'A diamond raid on Hatton Garden — that's how you read it, eh?'

'Yes — timed to coincide with Kesselring's coup. They couldn't have better timing, with the police out in force for the Presidential visit.'

Logan grinned. 'We'll be ready for them.' He swivelled round in his seat to look at me. 'You thought all along that there was something odd about Ellery being associated with Kesselring's group.'

'He didn't seem to fit, not in that set-up. I supposed that Kesselring was using him as a go-between with a handful of militant students. What I overheard makes it pretty clear that Ellery is also using Kesselring.'

'And now they're all waiting for the President's visit.' Logan shifted his weight. 'We don't even know when that is ourselves.'

'Weeks — a month?'

'Inside a month,' said Carruthers. 'As a matter of fact, we expect confirmation of a date from Washington any time now.'

'How strong will security be?'

'As strong as we can make it on our side — plus everything your fellow countrymen do, which will be considerable.' Carruthers hesitated, then said slowly: 'I don't like this situation, Shand.'

'Why not simply pull Kesselring and the rest in?' But even as I spoke I knew the answer.

Carruthers gave it, just the same. 'We'd do it, on any pretext we can invent — and we can do that all right — but for one thing.' He smiled thinly. 'We simply don't know where Kesselring is.'

'The whole thing could be called off, couldn't it?'

'It could — if the President was willing, but he isn't. We've been in daily contact with Washington and he's firm about it. Even if he did bow out we couldn't broadcast the real reason — and you can imagine the political repercussions.'

'Better a welter of international speculation than the death of a President of the United States,' mused Logan.

'The visit will take place, probably inside a fortnight,' Carruthers replied. 'We'll do our best to prevent an attempt on his life.'

'*If* there is one,' I said slowly.

Carruthers jerked his head round. 'I don't quite follow that, Shand.'

I didn't answer for a moment. I was remembering, as closely as I could get to it, the exact pattern of Kesselring's conversation in the villa at Ostia — the way he had started to boast in detail of what he planned and then suddenly changed direction. It had puzzled me at the time, but I had half forgotten it . . . until now.

'You've something else on your mind, Shand,' said Carruthers quietly.

'I'm just wondering if we've all been crediting Kesselring with the wrong motive.'

'Go on.'

'Before Kesselring left the villa he began boasting about their plans. Then, quite suddenly, he cut himself off, almost as if he was reluctant to reveal them even to people he expected to die the same night. It seemed odd, but I didn't really think about it until recently — until now, in fact.'

'And?'

'Just suppose this isn't an assassination plot under cover of an inspired riot. It could be something else.'

'What?'

'*Kidnapping — and ransom.*'

Carruthers was leaning forward in his chair, both hands splayed out on his desk. 'God Almighty, it's possible . . . '

'The President of the United States kidnapped — the ransom demand could be a million pounds. It could be anything they cared to ask. We've assumed throughout that this Corps One is being paid by enemies of the West to kill the President. But suppose they're acting independently — for the biggest prize-money imaginable?'

Carruthers breathed harshly down his nose. 'Yes, it's possible — but, dammit, the difficulties!'

'I agree. Kidnapping the most closely-guarded man on earth is tougher than trying to pick him off with a telescopic rifle — and that's not easy with hundreds of security fellows on hand.'

'A student riot of unprecedented violence might help,' reflected Logan.

'Kesselring boasted to me about enormous money,' I said. 'Well, I guess the fee for political murder could be on that scale. But, as I said, he suddenly quit talking about it, as though he had decided not to say any more. I like it best that they're going to snatch him.'

'Then he'll have to be guarded every waking and sleeping second of the day and night.'

'He might object — he might want to step out of the security line to talk with people. In any event, there'll be some occasions when he's alone . . . maybe a contrived opportunity.'

Carruthers nursed his moustache, almost agitatedly. 'If your theory is correct it's going to be *the* most hellish job we've ever handled.'

'There's a way of drawing their fire,' I said. 'An arranged leak of top security information.'

'Saying what?'

'A leak direct to Kesselring that the President is flying in earlier than expected and wishes his arrival to be *incognito* until he is actually in London.'

'I'm not quite with you, my dear chap. For one thing, how are we to get any sort of message through to Kesselring?'

'There are two other students linked with this underground movement. I think Ginny Leeming would be willing to see that they got any message we care to fabricate.'

'And they'll route it to one of the Kesselring's group?'

'I'm sure of it.'

Logan said: 'We could pull these young fellows in and grill them. They might not talk, though, eh?'

'No.' I looked round at them. 'Besides, it'll be a phony leak — *the President won't be here.*'

Carruthers stared. 'What's the point?'

'I'm suggesting complete but unannounced security measures . . . with a stand-in deputising for the President. A stand-in who knows what to expect — and is ready for it.'

'It's bizarre,' said Carruthers. His mouth twitched faintly. 'But it might work. And that way we catch them in the act.'

'That's what I have in mind.'

'The stand-in would have to be expertly made-up, enough to pass except at close quarters.'

'Naturally. But it could be done.'

Carruthers eyed me curiously. 'It'd be a bloody awful risk for the man who did it.'

'He'd take a calculated risk,' I said.

'Who would?'

'Me,' I said.

22

Two hours later I was on a Pan-Am jet for New York. Paula Vincent flew with me. All this was part of the plan.

I was to fly back the next day, impersonating the President travelling *incognito*. The phony tipoff through Ginny Leeming, who knew Phil Bennion, was put in hand before we left. In New York I was to see Carl Fiedler of the CIA for a general briefing and, finally, a facial disguise which would pass except at very close quarters.

Paula came with me because she was to be the link with the security men who would be near — but not so near as to make a kidnap coup impossible. A make-up man flown in from. Hollywood was to change her appearance, too — a light freckled tan, a severe blonde wig, tinted glasses.

Before we left Carruthers went through everything, point by point.

'We're *letting* you be kidnapped, Shand. Paula will be able to contact us by ultra-short wave personal radio.' He glanced across at her and added: 'Yours is a key job, Paula — you have to radio to us the exact route the kidnap car takes.'

'You could use police officers, Mr. Carruthers . . . '

'We could — but a woman is better, less likely even to be considered by the enemy.'

'Suppose I'm recognised?'

Carruthers allowed himself a faint smile. 'By the time you've been made-up even Shand himself will have small trouble in identifying you.'

'That sounds a bit uncomplimentary.'

'No, merely a tribute to the skill of the make-up man who will go to work on you.' He stood up. 'It is necessary for Shand to be actually kidnapped, under the impression that he is the President — then we close in and net the whole group.'

Paula put out a hand and closed it on mine. 'I'd better not slip up, then, had I?'

'You won't, Miss Vincent,' answered

Carruthers quietly.

We were airborne from Heathrow when she recalled his statement of confidence. 'Suppose I *do* fail!'

'Don't even think of it, Paula.'

'It's asking such a lot.'

'You know precisely what you have to do and how to do it. Everything's going to be all right.'

'God, I hope so. I'm so dreadfully worried. Not for myself — it's you I'm thinking of.'

I laughed. 'And when I first saw you I thought you were cool and disdainful!'

'That was just an act.' She moved closer to me in the seat. 'Why the hell did you agree to this mad thing?'

'Well, it was my idea to have a stand-in for the President and Carruthers liked it.'

'I didn't ask you that, I asked why did you ever offer to do it yourself.'

'I guess it was something I couldn't resist.'

'You've a successful business and make good money — why put your neck out like this?'

'I've taken chances before, Paula.'

'But not one like *this*!'

'Perhaps not so spectacular, but I've been in others no less dangerous. Most of the time the work I do is pretty dull routine, but every once in a while I go for some excitement, whether I'm paid or not. Anyway, I usually come out fairly well in the latter department. Besides, you won't fail me.'

'No,' she said in a low voice, 'I won't fail you.'

'Then what are you worrying about?'

'Everything — every single waking moment until it's all over. I've got about ten million butterflies in my tummy.'

'Let them drown in a large gin and tonic,' I said.

'This kind swim like crazy,' she answered.

We ate some of the seven-course dinner they put on for this flight. Neither of us could manage all of it. Time shrank, the way it does on the outward trip because you're flying into it. We talked, but not at length, and after a while relapsed into silence. Then the voice of the stewardess drifted down the pressurised cabin over the PA system:

'We shall be coming into Kennedy Airport in ten minutes. Will you please put out your cigarettes and fasten your seat belts. Captain Lewison and his crew hope you have enjoyed your flight . . . '

Through Customs and into a taxi pelting down the Van Wyck Expressway and on through the Queens Midtown Tunnel to Manhattan. A preliminary session with Carl Fiedler, a big handsome fellow in his early fifties with ash-grey hair and piercing dark eyes. Then another taxi — past Grand Central Station, skirting the theatre district and finally making the quiet square where Shand had his home all those years before settling in England.

I had been back to it once since then. The lease still had two years to run and I could have sub-let the apartment over and again, but I had never been able to bring myself to the point of cutting the last link. I guess Katie Allison was right when she told me on a never-to-be-forgotten night that I was an incurable romantic at heart.

On the other hand, why not keep a

piece of yourself in your native land? Some day I might want to come home for good. Meanwhile, it was pleasant to feel that you could fly to New York and step straight back into a place that belonged to you in a highly personal sense.

The plump smiling girl who had succeeded Nancy at the switchboard said: 'I managed to get the cleaning woman in to give your apartment a going-over, Mr. Shand.'

It was a warm night and one of the windows had been left half-open to the light breeze sighing in from the Battery — but you could still catch the faint mustiness of a place not lived in for a long time. I had a vague sense of letdown. It wasn't my home any longer, just a place to come to — how often? Once in twelve months. Maybe I had been wrong to keep it on?

Then Paula was saying: 'Why, Dale — it's nice here, I like it!'

'You're just saying that.'

She turned. 'No, that's not true. It's just not been lived in lately, that's all — but it's you all right.'

I looked round. Everything *was* the same, fundamentally. The rust-red carpet, the deep easy chairs, the desk ranged against the window. The bookshelves still housing the authors I read and often re-read — Shakespeare, Maugham, Trollope, Dickens, Chandler, O'Hara, Jane Austen and P. G. Wodehouse. On the lower shelf, stacked vertically, long-playing albums of Armstrong, the Condon mob, Teagarden, Pee Wee and Muggsy Spanier. The last three gone now, along with too many more who created the kind of music that will live until the last trumpet note fades and dies in the last jazz cellar. Everything the way I had left it, like a mute extension of whatever personality I have, an integral part of Shand. Yet, in some faintly disturbing way, I felt partially outside it. Quite suddenly, it came to me that this was no longer my home, that I belonged now in England. If I belonged anywhere. I wasn't sure of that, either.

'You know what this place needs?' said Paula. 'It needs the smell of tobacco. No, not cigarettes — a pipe.'

I lit it and went to the sideboard and found an unopened bottle of Scotch.

Paula said: 'It's all terribly masculine.' She laughed and held out both arms to me. 'Take the pipe from your mouth first.'

I held her against my body, aware of what the warm physical contact was doing to me. Then she pulled away and asked: 'Where are we going tonight?'

'To Marty Alton's club.'

'Who's Marty Alton?'

'A friend. A disgustingly rich friend who runs a club because that's what he likes doing with his life. More specifically, because it enables him to hire the kind of small jazz groups he loves hearing.'

'I don't really know much about jazz, but I'm willing to go anywhere you want to go,' she said. 'First, though, I'm going to take a shower and change my clothes. You just relax with a glass in your hand and smoke that old pipe.'

'All right.' But first I called Marty and fixed a table reservation.

We got there shortly after nine o'clock. He was waiting in the small foyer, a compact smiling man with a fresh complexion who looked as if he had never found life anything less than agreeable. 'Dale — this is an occasion,' he said. His gaze went appreciatively to Paula.

'Miss Paula Vincent,' I said. 'Paula to you.'

'It is a pleasure to meet you, Paula,' said Marty, holding her hand rather longer than seemed strictly necessary. Hell, you're not jealous, Shand? Yes.

We had drinks in the private office. Marty eyed me thoughtfully and said: 'Are you over on private or professional business — or shouldn't I inquire?'

'Mainly professional. I'll tell you about it — but not now. Next time I'm here.'

'You might have an earlier opportunity — I'm thinking of opening a similar club in London.'

'Are you being serious?'

'Very. I'm already in negotiation for a place just off Regent Street. As a matter of fact. I'm going over to London next week.'

'Well,' said Paula, 'there's one thing certain — you'll have at least two customers.'

'I'll look forward to that,' Marty replied. 'And now, permit me to show you to your table.' He cupped Paula's elbow and led the way buoyantly with old man Shand bringing up in the rear, which is something that invariably happens any time I take a pretty girl into Marty's club.

The band cut loose on *Sister Kate*, the up-tempo version with the front line driving hard against the subtle lift of a rhythm section whose drummer laid down the kind of Chicago beat I hadn't heard since Dave Tough was around. They rode out the *coda* and after a few minutes went into the *Beale Street Blues* — slow and relaxed with the trombone man delivering the ceaselessly flowing phrases Jack Teagarden used to do. Everything quiet and low-down . . . the indescribably moving nuances of the twelve-bar blues, strangely evocative, simultaneously exuberant and melancholy. Paula liked this, too.

It was coming up to eleven-fifty when we left. The night was still fine and warm and she asked if we could walk home.

I shook my head. 'Better not. This town

isn't the safest place for pedestrians at night. We might get mugged, especially if we stroll along Forty-second Street.'

'Mugged — what's that mean?'

'Attacked from behind and robbed, almost certainly beaten up.'

She said: 'It's a violent city, isn't it?'

'It's a violent country, though there are still millions of us living hometown lives. Decent folk who hate all the things they read about in the newspapers and see on television.'

'Yes.' She answered meditatively. 'It's getting that way in England, especially in the cities. What's gone wrong with everything, Dale?'

'A sickness in society itself. A lot of factors — the frustrations and anarchy of the young, the false idea that material prosperity inevitably means social and moral progress. Above all, the rise of evil.'

'That's an old-fashioned word.'

'A lot of old-fashioned things are coming true, Paula.' I flagged down a taxi and we drove home. The apartment house was in darkness except for the light in the reception foyer. We walked up the stairs hand in hand and turned into the first floor corridor.

We were rounding the small bend when I stopped. The door to my apartment was half-opened and light came from the lounge.

Paula put her mouth close up to my ear. 'I'll go in ahead of you . . . '

I shook my head, gripping her arm.

'Please — if there's anything wrong it's the best way. Then you come in with the advantage of surprise.' Even as she breathed the words she pulled her arm free and went in.

I couldn't have stopped her without betraying sound, but I didn't like it. I walked on and stood against the wall to the side of the partly open door.

The voice of a man, and I knew him — Bowles.

'Well, if it's not pretty baby — come right in and make yourself at home.'

Paula said: 'What are you doing here?'

'Waiting for Shand. I might ask you the same question, only there's a better one — like *where* is he?'

'Downstairs. He'll be here in a few minutes and throw you out.'

'Yeah?' He laughed. 'When the gum-shoe walks in it'll be the last thing he ever does.'

That meant Bowles had a gun out, a silenced gun — or a knife. No, it would be a gun.

He went on: 'Knew you'd flown to New York, sweetheart — you and him both. We had guys watching the airport. Kesselring figures Shand is joining the guard on the President when he flies out tomorrow.'

Paula invented a startled exclamation.

'You didn't know we were on to that, did you?' jeered Bowles. 'Baby, we know everything. Not that it'd make any difference Shand joining the security set-up. We got it all made.'

'Then why are you here?'

'Just to make sure the President is on the plane tomorrow. Then I send a cable to an address in Stepney and it's routed to Kesselring. It's written out ready, right here in my pocket, sweetheart. But there's one other thing . . . ' He paused, savouring the words to come. Then: 'Something even Kesselring doesn't know. I got the idea on the way over. I'm going to finish Shand — you, too, baby. Put you both out of the way, is all. When Shand walks in, that'll be it.'

A sound, as if he had got up from a chair. 'Kesselring will be pleased,' he said.

I went softly back down the corridor, raced to street level and reached the fire stairs. They went up past my bedroom window. The cleaning woman had left that half-open, too. I stepped in, tiptoed across the carpet and poked at the door.

Bowles was standing with his back towards me, covering the way in from the corridor.

'What's keeping him? There's something . . .'

I slammed the door wide open. He heard the sound and wheeled completely round. Paula swung her handbag down on his hand, the .45 Navy Colt hit the floor and I tore into the room, diving headlong for his legs. We rolled over and over in silent savagery; came up on our feet, locked in clawing combat. He pulled away, no more than inches but enough to go for a knife. He got it out fast, crouching to slash it upwards, the two movements fusing almost like one. I brought my right foot up in a single kick to the jaw.

He shot straight back, turning torment-edly like a spinning top, blood gushing from his mouth. But he still had the knife. I started to close in before he could come at me — but it wasn't necessary.

Paula said coolly: 'Drop it, drop that knife!'

He lurched, staring madly. She was aiming the .45 at one of the less agreeable places in which to receive a bullet.

*   *   *

I called Fiedler and they came and took Bowles away.

'This fellow is wanted for murder three times over,' Carl Fiedler said. 'Two in Chicago and another out in L.A.'

'Better not charge him in open court, not just yet,' I said.

Fiedler smiled. 'I have that firmly in

mind. We'll let his buddies in England figure everything's swell, eh?'

'Yes.' I looked at the cable form I had taken from Bowles and handed it over.

Fiedler said: 'I'll have it sent the moment the plane takes off.' He held out a strong, firm hand. 'You're our kind of guy, Shand — good luck tomorrow.'

'I'll need it,' I said.

23

The plane came into Heathrow at 2100 hours. I had travelled with three of Carl Fiedler's men, and several seats away from Paula and the rest of the passengers. The makeup boffin had changed her all right, without any over-elaboration.

They had changed me, too. I had seen myself in a full-length mirror — different clothes, different bearing and, above all, a skilled difference in facial appearance. The contrived resemblance wasn't final, never could be; but maybe it was enough to deceive the kidnappers, more especially as Kesselring wasn't going to be there when it took place — Bowles had let that out under preliminary questioning. Where would he be? Well I was going to find out . . .

No Customs formalities. Straight into the VIP lounge, not staying there. Out to the waiting car, a Humber Imperial with diplomatic insignia. Then down through the tunnel and out on to the traffic-crowded road thrusting into the heart of London. There was a slight dampness in the palms of my hands.

The Intelligence man who was with me said: 'It's not going to be easy — deliberately letting them take you. If we make it too obvious they'll suspect something.'

'Unless I've guessed wrong, there'll be one hell of a demonstration going on when we hit Grosvenor Square,' I said. 'That's when it'll happen, giving them the confusion and cover they need.'

There were two other cars, ahead and behind us, carrying British security men. All armed. Not that they were going to need fire-power in Grosvenor Square. Later perhaps. Paula was driving a third car, not too close to the motorcade.

The radio telephone came on. It was Carruthers. 'How are you feeling, Mr. President?' He might have been chatting me up at a garden party.

'Lousy.'

'Nervous anticipation, eh? That's fine — shows you're keyed-up for the job. I hear they made quite an achievement with your face.'

'It'll not fool Kesselring.'

'Doesn't have to. By the time he sees you he'll be seeing us.'

'I hope so.'

'We'll be there,' he said comfortably. 'By the way, you were right about there being a demonstration. It's already beginning to look like a gigantic rugger scrum. See you . . .'

The instrument clicked into silence. I stared at it, sweating.

Then we were moving into the square — and the sweat and the tension and the inner doubts vanished, like a total wipe in a motion picture film. I felt the two weapons I was carrying — a .22 target pistol and a slim gun which sprayed a temporarily paralysing gas. Very effective, according to Fiedler. But you had to have the opportunity to use it. Was I going to have the chance? We'll see.

The entire square was in turmoil, massed bodies surging against the line of uniformed police outside the Embassy. Mounted men cleared a way for the cars and we edged forward.

No ambush, no shots from a rooftop sniper. The crowd was split up into banner-carrying platoons, chanting familiar catch-phrases. Over to the left a crowd of young fellows and girls were involved in a scuffle with the police and several of them were bundled into a black van. It was just routine — so far.

I looked out of the right-hand window, trying to figure where the attack was going to come from. Something *had* to happen now, within minutes.

Suddenly, a yell went up from a section of the demonstrators thrusting behind a banner proclaiming *Students' and People's Democracy* — *Action Not Words!*

'It's the President!'

The yell was repeated by a score of voices. A big bearded man who looked years past university age shouted: '*Now!*'

This was it, an arranged signal. A solid wedge of bodies thrust forward, then fanned out in a drilled line. The car began to rock . . . in another moment the offside wheels were lifting and the car toppled completely over. The driver was trapped. Then the nearside door was wrenched open and hands reached in to drag me clear. They belonged to a tall man in a dark suit who said calmly: 'We'll get you safely into another car — this way, sir.'

A second man appeared, reaching inside the overturned vehicle. I heard a single dull thud and he said: 'Your guard seems to be hurt, but he'll be all right.'

The car in front had half-turned. I got in, the two men sitting on either side of me. The door shut and the driver swung at an angle. People started jumping out of its way and two of them were sent flying. The rest fell back, opening a path.

Police began to swarm in — but now the car was gathering speed. In another moment it was out of the square. I looked through the rear window.

Paula's car was following.

Then everything was blotted out as a hood was jammed down over my head and I was slammed to the floor.

A muffled voice said: 'Don't try to get up, Mr. President — you can't see it, but there's a gun looking at you.'

I fingered the watch strapped on my left wrist — only it wasn't a watch. One of Carruthers' gimmicks, a subminiature radio transmitter.

'What is the meaning of this . . . this outrage?' My words sounded like something out of old-fashioned melodrama.

Another voice: 'Don't waste time on him, Hans.'

'Why not? I enjoy talking to the President of the United States. It's a new experience.'

I said: 'Where are you taking me?'

'Just say you're going on a little unscheduled trip, Mr. President.'

'I demand an explanation . . . '

'You'll get one when we reach Askam Cutting.' The voice made a deep chuckle. 'Not that you'll know where that is.'

I cut the tiny transmitter out. I hoped Paula had got the message.

★   ★   ★

We had left the road. Now the car wheels were crunching on soft, uneven ground. That meant we were on the bank, nearing the cutting. Then we were there, going into a building. Doors closed and electric light came on; I could tell that even through the hood.

The man called Hans said cosily: 'Journey's end, Mr. President. If you will please step from the car.'

I groped my way out. Hands gripped both both my arms, propelling me — where? Into a room of some kind. I was pushed down in a chair. The hood had been fastened round my neck and I put hands up to it.

'Not yet, Mr. President. That task will be performed for you — presently.' He laughed. 'The pleasure is being specially reserved for your host. Louis will stay with you in the meantime . . . '

He went away. Minutes passed, never more slowly. I had the trick gun holstered on my left thigh — but I couldn't risk even touching it, not yet. Louis was probably looking directly at me.

I said: 'There'll be a price to pay for this, my friend.'

'That's right — a big one.'

'You'll never get away with this.'

'Shut up,' he snarled.

Then the door opened and a remembered voice said: 'Welcome Mr. President.'

It was Kesselring.

Louis said: 'Don't you want to see him?'

'In a few moments. There is no hurry. Our distinguished guest can amuse himself wondering what I look like.'

Footsteps neared and Hans said: 'Well, we've done it, Chief.'

'No trouble?'

'No, except that Louis had to knock out the Yank who was with him in the car. Apart from that, everything went like clockwork, as the British say.'

Kesselring said: 'You've done well. There'll be a bonus. What about the security cars?'

'They took *us* for security. We had the markings. They didn't even approach us.'

A small silence, then Kesselring again: 'You're quite positive about this, Hans?'

'But of course. Why?'

'It sounds almost too easy,' Kesselring answered. He laughed. 'On the other hand, our planning was perfect.'

'I told you — everything went like clockwork. The inspired student riot, one section clashing with the coppers while the second overturned the car . . . then we moved in to rescue the President.'

Another voice — Svendstrom's. 'The small body of militant students co-operated admirably.' He chuckled. 'Also unwittingly in the sense that they imagine Corps One to be a revolutionary movement dedicated to the overthrowing of the capitalist system.'

'Dedicated to plundering it would be more apt, eh? How fortunate that the students are unaware that you killed one of their eager colleagues, my dear Svendstrom.'

'It was imperative — he was becoming suspicious.'

'But of course — I ordered it myself. Everything else has proceeded with the utmost simplicity, which is always the best strategy. There *was* one little unforeseen problem, though.'

It was Lapete who answered. '*Oui, m'sieu* . . . it was most fortunate that we were able to surmount it.'

Kesselring raised his voice slightly. 'This you must hear, Mr. President. You were almost truly rescued. The police actually followed our car. But we were more than their match.'

I said nothing. No matter how I tried to disguise my voice it wouldn't deceive Kesselring.

'You are plunged into silence, Mr. President,' he mocked. 'Yes, there were two police cars not far behind us. I should explain that by this time I myself had joined the procession — in the forefront, naturally. I confess I found the presence of these representative of the law a little puzzling, since *we* were supposed to be conducting you to safety. You are listening, I hope, Mr. President?'

I nodded.

Kesselring resumed: 'They were not smart enough to be really close. In fact, they stupidly allowed some girl motorist to get between them and us. However, thanks to the meticulous detail of our planning, all was well. At a suitable point one of our colleagues merely drove a truck out of a side street, effectively blocking them off — an added precaution we had not expected to use but nevertheless held in readiness. And now you are our guest, quite beyond all hope of resuming the responsibilities of office until the appropriate reward — or should I say ransom? — has been paid.' A pause, then: 'We shall ask the Government of the United States for the dollar equivalent of two million pounds sterling.'

A match flared, the air was fragrant with Havana cigar smoke. Kesselring said: 'Now — let us contemplate our distinguished guest, eh?'

I could hear him move forward. Fingers released the fastening and the hood was swept upwards over my face. He stepped back. For a fraction of time the transition from darkness to light was almost dazzling. Then I saw them grouped in front of me — Kesselring, Svendstrom and Lapete in the centre of four others.

Hans said: 'Well, there he is, Chief . . . '

Kesselring had dropped his cigar. He was standing with his head thrust oddly forward, the pupils of his eyes dilated. The sudden silence in the room was almost tangible, like something you could reach out and grasp.

Then he literally screamed.

'Fools, dolts! This man is not . . . ' He closed in, his face no more than inches from mine. He straightened up, slowly, going backwards. A single word came from him.

'*Shand*!'

Lapete said in a shrill voice: 'It . . . it can't be . . . '

Kesselring stood there, looking down at me. When he spoke again his voice had modulated to a deadly whisper. 'The disguise is brilliant . . . that is to say, brilliant for a limited purpose.'

Hans, a huge lumbering man with a face like wet putty, started to mumble something. Kesselring waved a hand. 'I am not blaming you or Louis. You had to carry out the abduction swiftly and in in conditions which permitted no detailed observation. Nor could you anticipate that there would be a changeling . . . *stand up, Mr. Shand*!'

I didn't and Kesselring's hand jumped out, lashing me across the jaw.

His heavy mouth twisted. 'Where have they taken the President?'

'Nowhere . . . *you*'ve been taken for the ride, Kesselring.'

He staggered back as if he had been struck. 'You . . . you mean he isn't here, in this country?'

'If you want him you'll have to go to the White House, but I wouldn't recommend it.'

Kesselring stood there, utterly without movement, like a stone man. Then he began to laugh, a macabre parody of mirth.

When he stopped, Svendstrom said: 'Now I kill him for you. Most slowly. Not the quick push under the train or the death I give to the girl . . . '

He broke off as Lapete slid a long knife into his hand.

'I am the executioner,' Svendstrom said softly.

Kesselring made his appalling laugh again, briefly. 'Not just yet, my friends.' The ravaged features were composed now, the voice quiet and unhurried. Only the eyes betrayed the pathological hate which engulfed him.

'Two million pounds . . . the greatest coup of all time.' He seemed to be whispering the words to himself.

I said: 'You overlooked one simple thing — any two can play.'

'Go on, Mr. Shand — while you still have the chance. You will not have it much longer, I do assure you.'

I started talking, not because it mattered that he should know. I was buying myself time. Not much time, but a little. 'Intelligence worked first on the assumption that you were planning political assassination. Something you said, or, rather left unsaid in Italy made me think you might be out for the world's biggest prize — the ransom for a President.'

A blood vessel pulsed high on his left temple. 'You have no conception of how long it is going to take you to die, Mr. Shand . . . '

'But not here, Kesselring?'

'No, my cruiser is moored in the cutting. It is of ocean-going capacity. We shall take you back to Ostia. Incidentally, you have yet to inform us how you eluded Belligi ... ' He stopped again. 'It is strange that we have had no word from that one. Or perhaps not so strange. He will fear the punishment his carelessness so richly merits.'

'He's beyond your reach, Kesselring. The shark ate him instead of me.'

'I will kill him — now!' breathed Svendstrom.

'No.' Kesselring held up a hand. His eyes glittered at me. 'You shall tell us more of that later, Mr. Shand. But you were saying?'

'I said any two can play. All we had to do was to create a situation in which you believed the President was coming here *incognito* ... and plant a stand-in,' I forced a grin. 'Corps One — nine men dreaming-up a coup without precedent in history. Only you forgot the tenth man.'

'*You!*' Kesselring began to shake. Froth bubbled on his thick mouth. 'You bloody, bloody American ... ' He half-choked on the words. Then he got a grip on himself. 'The police ... '

Svendstrom grated: 'They do not know where we are.'

'They'll find out.' Kesselring went to the door, listening. There were no sounds from beyond it. 'That is, they'll find us if we stay.' He turned. 'Put Shand in the cruiser . . . we leave now!'

Lapete snarled: 'Move, *m'sieu*. If you attempt the escape it will be most pleasurable to put the knife in your back.'

We went through the door and out on to a short landing-stage and into the cruiser. Svendstrom took his grotesque straw hat off and hit me sideways across the mouth with the brim. I could taste the salty tang of blood.

One of the others put his foot in the small of my back as I went down the short companion-way and sent me sprawling into a cabin. I landed on my hands and knees, sliding across the floor as the door closed.

Then the motor pulsed into life and the cruiser started to move, nosing out from the landing-stage and going down the cutting for the open river.

I jerked the zip of my pants wide open

and got the trick-gun out. If they came for me I could take them now — well some of them. Not all nine, though. I could hear them on the deck. Kesselring's voice rose above the others.

'When we reach the river just cruise steadily downstream, Lapete — do not attract attention to us.'

'*Oui* — I understand.'

Svendstrom said loudly: 'We should kill this man Shand now. Not wait till we return to Italy.'

It seemed like a full minute before Kesselring answered. I could hear the wash of the water as the cruiser gathered speed. Then he said: 'Yes. If by some ill-chance we are stopped there will then be no Shand and thus no evidence. Yes, kill him Svendstrom ... but not too rapidly.'

The Swede laughed evilly. 'I know many ways. His screams will be music, eh?'

Footsteps. Then, quite suddenly, a new sound — the distant throb of engines. The footsteps ceased.

Lapete screeched: 'Police launches

. . . they are heading into the cutting . . . '

I moved fast across the cabin, away from the door. It burst open. Kesselring was framed in it — his face a collapsed ruin, almost insane.

He wheeled as I triggered the gun. The gas spray took him right in the mouth. He made a strangled croak and his legs telescoped under him. Then he went straight down, his face grinding into the floor.

That still left Svendstrom. He lunged in at an angle and turned with a long slim dagger in his right hand. I jumped sideways as he threw it. The blade drove into the wall, the handle quivering.

I went after him with my bare hands. He danced aside, his empty hand making a sweeping curve. A .38 jumped into it — but in the same instant I rammed him head-first in the belly. He shot back as if he had been hit by a slammed door. The gun spun from him. I grabbed it, turned it in my hand as he bounced off the other wall and laid the solid butt on his bull-neck with a chunky thud.

He went down like a tenpin in a

bowling alley, spread-eagled and unseeing. I held the gun pointing down, a finger flexing on the trigger. For a moment in time I knew the urge to murder — an almost overmastering compulsion to kill the man who had broken Amanda Chester's neck.

Outside the cabin the air was charged with a pandemonium of sound — the zoom of circling river patrol launches, the judder of braked cars on the bank, shouted commands, panic voices and the splash of bodies diving into the water. But they weren't going to escape.

I looked down at Svendstrom, at the gun in my hand. I opened my fingers and let it slide to the floor.

Footsteps thudded heavily on the deck. A voice shouted: 'Are you all right, Shand?' It was Carruthers.

I called to them, starting for the short companion-way as lighter footsteps came down it.

'I came right on the deadline, didn't I?' said Paula. She looked down at my front and added: 'Better fasten yourself up before Mr. Carruthers walks in . . . you look positively indecent . . . '

★ ★ ★

They found enough documented evidence to put Kesselring, Svendstrom and Lapete away for as long as they were likely to live.

A concealed network of espionage covering nine countries. Some very unexpected collaborators in high places on the Continent. Contacts both in London and New York.

The Corps One dossier was explicit and definitive, fingering a dozen supposedly irreproachable names.

We were all assembled in Carruthers' elegant office and the new Minister was with us.

Carruthers said: 'You ought to join us permanently, my dear Shand.' He smiled faintly. 'On second thoughts, perhaps not — you function best as a lone wolf. Well, not always entirely alone.' His quizzical gaze went to Paula and back to me. 'By the way, the President is pleased. He

310

wishes to meet you when you go to the States, which I assume will be almost immediately?'

'Probably within two days. The industrial assignment I'm handling takes in Washington.'

'Everything fits admirably.' He gave me his strong hand. 'We'll look forward to your working with us again some time I hope.'

I grinned. 'Not if I can see it coming.'

'I don't believe that, my dear fellow,' said Carruthers imperturbably, 'Oh, by the way, you'll be delighted to know that Logan's team caught your friend Garfield Ellery and his chums in the act. A quarter of a million pounds in diamonds. You were right about that, too. You're really rather a remarkable chap, you know.'

'No, I didn't.'

'I did,' said Paula cryptically.

I flew to New York three hours after the briefing at Jack Kennings' riverside home. A nice dull routine job paying lots of nice but not dull money. No violence and not much intrigue, only the power game kind. Very damned dull. I was going to love it.

311

It was nine in the evening when I got to my old apartment. I used the stairs, remembering how I had walked up them hand in hand with Paula. Remembering a lot of things. It was lonely without her.

I turned into the corridor and stopped abruptly. Light was showing under my door exactly as it had showed before. Not *another* fellow with a forty-five . . . nobody could possibly be gunning for me now. Better be sure, though. I kicked the door and went fast to one side.

A voice.

'Come in, Dale . . . '

I stepped through and she was standing there in powder-blue *négligé* with her arms out.

All I could think of to say was: 'What the hell are *you* doing here?'

'I've joined the British Intelligence,' she said calmly. 'Mr. Carruthers said that if he couldn't have you he was damned well going to have me.'

'I damned well hope not!'

'I didn't mean it that way and you know it,' said Paula.

'You still haven't said what you're

doing over here.'

'Mr. Carruthers wants me to link-up with the Central Intelligence Agency on a sort of lease-lend mission.' She made her small gurgling laugh. 'I'd have come, anyway.'

'What for?'

'You shouldn't need to ask that.' She came close in against me. Her long mouth sought mine. She said: 'You're trembling.'

'God damn it, what do you expect?' I held her from me with both hands and said: 'You have an uncanny knack of turning up at exactly the right time.'

'That's right,' she answered. 'I'm the original deadline dolly.'

I laughed. 'I've never thought of you as a dolly.'

'How *have* you thought of me?'

'Do you really want to know?'

'Yes, please.'

I took her hand and walked with her towards the door to the side of the lounge.

It was already open . . .

We do hope that you have enjoyed reading this large print book.

Did you know that all of our titles are available for purchase?

We publish a wide range of high quality large print books including:
Romances, Mysteries, Classics
General Fiction
Non Fiction and Westerns

Special interest titles available in large print are:
The Little Oxford Dictionary
Music Book, Song Book
Hymn Book, Service Book

Also available from us courtesy of Oxford University Press:
Young Readers' Dictionary
(large print edition)
Young Readers' Thesaurus
(large print edition)

For further information or a free brochure, please contact us at:
Ulverscroft Large Print Books Ltd.,
The Green, Bradgate Road, Anstey,
Leicester, LE7 7FU, England.
Tel: (00 44) **0116 236 4325**
Fax: (00 44) **0116 234 0205**

DEATH CALLED AT NIGHT

R. A. Bennett

Jimmy Ellis believes his parents have died in a car crash when as a young boy he is taken to live with relatives in Australia. The years pass happily, then the nightmare comes. Terrifying images flit through his mind in the dark — all through the eyes of a child, a witness to grisly events seventeen years before. He begins to delve into the past, and soon he finds himself on the trail of a double murderer — a murderer who is prepared to kill again.

THE DEAD TALE-TELLERS

John Newton Chance

Jonathan Blake always kept appointments. He had kept many, in all sorts of places, at all sorts of times, but never one like that one he kept in the house in the woods in the fading light of an October day. It seemed a perfect, peaceful place to visit and perhaps take tea and muffins round the fire. But at this appointment his footsteps dragged, for he knew that inside the house the men with whom he had that date were already dead . . .

TURN DOWN AN EMPTY GLASS

Basil Copper

L.A. private detective Mike Faraday is plunged into a bizarre web of Haitian voodoo and murder when the beautiful singer Jenny Lundquist comes to him in fear for her life. Staked out at the lonely Obelisk Point, Mike sees the sinister Legba, the voodoo god of the cross-roads, with his cane and straw sack. But Mike discovers that beneath the superstition and an apparently motiveless series of appalling crimes is an ingenious plot — with a multi-million dollar prize.

DEATH IN RETREAT

George Douglas

On a day of retreat for clergy at Overdale House, a resident guest, Martin Pender, is foully murdered. The primary task of the Regional Homicide Squad is to track down the bogus parson who joined the retreat. Subsequent events show that serious political motives lie behind the killing, but the basic lead to it all is missing. Then, three young tearaways corner the killer in the woods, and a chess problem, set out on a board, yields vital evidence.

THE DEAD DON'T SCREAM

Leonard Gribble

Why had a woman screamed in Knightsbridge? Anthony Slade, the Yard's popular Commander of X2, sets out to investigate. Furthering the same end is Ken Surridge, a PR executive from a Northern consortium. Like Slade, Surridge wants to know why financier Shadwell Staines was shot and why a very scared girl appeared wearing a woollen housecoat. Before any facts can be discovered the girl takes off and Surridge gives chase, with Slade hot on his heels . . .

THE MURDER MAKERS

John Newton Chance

Julian Hammer wrote thrillers. When people asked him how he thought of all the murders, he would reply that he did them personally first. Thus, when Jonathan Blake called on Hammer to look into the case of a missing person, it did appear that the author might have killed him. Hammer, twisting by habit, twisted the issue so well Blake began to suspect that it was Hammer who was in line to be murdered. But Hammer thought it was likely to be Blake. Both were dead right.